Samuel French Acting Edition

AF278370

The Sparkley Clean Funeral Singers

Book by
Lori Fischer

Music & Lyrics by
Lori Fischer and Don Chaffer

SAMUELFRENCH.COM   SAMUELFRENCH.CO.UK

FOR PRODUCTION ENQUIRIES

UNITED STATES AND CANADA
Info@SamuelFrench.com
1-866-598-8449

UNITED KINGDOM AND EUROPE
Plays@SamuelFrench.co.uk
020-7255-4302

Each title is subject to availability from Samuel French, depending upon country of performance. Please be aware that *THE SPARKLEY CLEAN FUNERAL SINGERS* may not be licensed by Samuel French in your territory. Professional and amateur producers should contact the nearest Samuel French office or licensing partner to verify availability.

MUSIC USE NOTE

Licensees are solely responsible for obtaining formal written permission from copyright owners to use copyrighted music in the performance of this play and are strongly cautioned to do so. If no such permission is obtained by the licensee, then the licensee must use only original music that the licensee owns and controls. Licensees are solely responsible and liable for all music clearances and shall indemnify the copyright owners of the play(s) and their licensing agent, Samuel French, against any costs, expenses, losses and liabilities arising from the use of music by licensees. Please contact the appropriate music licensing authority in your territory for the rights to any incidental music.

IMPORTANT BILLING AND CREDIT REQUIREMENTS

If you have obtained performance rights to this title, please refer to your licensing agreement for important billing and credit requirements.

THE SPARKLEY CLEAN FUNERAL SINGERS was originally commissioned by Stacia Fernandez and received its southern premiere in 2016 at Cumberland County Playhouse; Producing Director/CEO Bryce McDonald, Artistic Director Britt Hancock, direction by Bryce McDonald, musical direction by Ron Murphy, and stage management by Kayla Jenkins, with the following cast:

JUNIE LASHLEY......................................Lori Fischer
LASHLEY LEE LASHLEY............................. Weslie Webster
PASTOR PHIL.......................................Britt Hancock
LYLE E. LASHLEY.. Bill Frey

THE SPARKLEY CLEAN FUNERAL SINGERS received its world premiere in 2013 at Capital Repertory Theatre; Producing Artistic Director Maggie Mancinelli-Cahill, direction by Martha Banta, musical direction by Don Chaffer, and stage management by Ashley Dumas, with the following cast:

JUNIE LASHLEY......................................Lori Fischer
LASHLEY LEE LASHLEY ....Carter Calvert
PASTOR PHIL...................................... Jesse Lenat
LYLE E. LASHLEY..................................Reathel Bean

For more information on recording any of these songs, please contact the authors. Relevant mechanical or synchronisation licenses are represented by Lori Fischer for Lori Fischer, and by either Simpleville Music or Don Chaffer for Don Chaffer.

CHARACTERS

2 WOMEN/2 MEN

JUNIE LASHLEY – Optimistic, yet curiously obsessed with/afraid of death, very funny, kind, ambitious, loves to sing, but petrified to sing alone, strong actress, comedienne and singer, 40s

LASHLEY LEE LASHLEY – Funny, attractive, sexy, alcoholic, feels a constant inner ache from having been abandoned by her mom, strong singer and actress, 40s

LYLE E. LASHLEY – Junie and Lashley's father, deeply in love with his estranged wife, has Alzheimer's, loves his daughters and loves to sing, late 60s/early 70s

PASTOR PHIL – Gambling addict, very funny, sincere, singer and compulsive hugger, big time Lashley Sisters fan, 35–40

SETTING

Ashland City, Tennessee

Sparkley Clean Dry Cleaners

Lashley Family Kitchen

Third United Separated Harmony Church

A Crappy Hotel Room

TIME

The Prologue takes place on the night of April 16, 2008. The rest of the play takes place during the weeks of May 5–19, 2008.

AUTHOR'S NOTES

You stack one more day on top of one more night.
It takes a lot of small steps to build a beautiful life…

MUSICAL NUMBERS

Act One

1. Honky Without the Tonky
2. Back at the Sparkley
3. Death is Everywhere
4. Big Time Plans
5. Bindy, Take a Seat at the Banquet Table ('Cause There's No Need for Food Drives in Heaven)
6. No Impulse Control
7. Sweet Macaroon
8. Love Hangs On
9. Humdinger Sing Along
10. Jimmy Boy Brown and His Toy Poodle, Puddin'
11. Begin and End With You

Act Two

12. St. Peter, If You're Listening, Tell Arthur Reid Hello
13. A Little Bitty Bug Bit a Little Bitty Bear
14. All You Can Eat Liver and Onions
15. Alcoholic Bungee Jumper
16. Sweet Macaroon (Reprise)
17. Hello to Another Goodbye
18. Lay Your Burden Down
19. To Build a Beautiful Life (A Poem for My Daughters)

Special Thanks to

Dramatists Guild, Florida Studio Theatre Richard and Betty Burdick Play Reading Series, The York Theatre Co. Reading Series, Simpleville Music, Helen Vaskevitch, Ed Stern, Christopher Allen, Lori Coscia Chaffer, Helen and Bob Fischer, Eduardo Machado, and Marsha Norman

PROLOGUE

(Concert lights flash around the stage.)

VOICEOVER. And now, put your hands together for *The Lashley Sisters*!

(Sound of applause.)

*(**JUNIE LASHLEY** takes the back-up singer mic as her sister, **LASHLEY LASHLEY**, takes the center stage/lead singer mic.)*

[MUSIC NO.1 "HONKY WITHOUT THE TONKY"]

LASHLEY.

DARLIN',

JUNIE.

HE CALLED HER –

LASHLEY.

DARLIN', YOU'RE THE ONE I'VE BEEN WAITING FOR.

JUNIE.

EVIDENTLY, HE'D BEEN SINGLE FOR A WHILE.

LASHLEY.

WHEN I'M WITH YOU, MY HEART'S AN OPEN DOOR.

JUNIE.

HE PULLED HER CLOSE AND SAID:

LASHLEY.

I'M FEELIN' THINGS I NEVER FELT BEFORE.

JUNIE.

THEN HE SAID,

LASHLEY.

HEAVEN, WE'RE HEADED FOR HEAVEN.
EACH KISS ITS OW-OWN CONVERSA-A-A-TION.

JUNIE.

OO, THEY HAD A LOT TO TALK ABOUT!

LASHLEY.

EACH TOUCH A SENSUAL CELEBRATION.

JUNIE.

OO, KIND OF LIKE A CONSTANT PAID VACATION!

LASHLEY.

YOU EASE MY MIND FROM ALL FRUSTRATION. THAT'S WHY
IT'S SAD,

JUNIE.

HE SAID,

LASHLEY.

SO VERY SAD,

JUNIE.

HE SAID,

LASHLEY.

IT MAKES ME SAD,

JUNIE.

HE SAID,

LASHLEY.

YOU'RE ALL I NEED, BUT I HAVE TO LEAVE!

JUNIE.

HE SAID WHAT?

LASHLEY.

I HAVE TO LEAVE.

JUNIE. Well, what good is that?

LASHLEY. Yeah.

LASHLEY & JUNIE.

WHAT GOOD IS THAT?

LASHLEY.

THAT'S LIKE THE HONKY,

JUNIE.

HONKY!

LASHLEY.

WITHOUT THE TONKY,

JUNIE.

  TONKY!

LASHLEY.

  LIKE THE

JUNIE & LASHLEY.

  THUNDER WITHOUT THE RAI-AY-AY-AY-AY-AIN,

LASHLEY.

  LIKE A THEORY

JUNIE.

  THEORY,

LASHLEY.

  WITHOUT A QUERY

JUNIE.

  QUERY,

JUNIE & LASHLEY.

  AN EXPLANATION THAT YOU CAN'T EXPLAIN.
  THAT'S LIKE THE BOOGIE WITHOUT THE WHOAH, WHOAH
     WOOGIE,
  LIKE AN ANGEL WITH JUST ONE WING.

LASHLEY.

  IT'S LIKE THE OCEAN,

JUNIE.

  OCEAN,

LASHLEY.

  WITHOUT THE

JUNIE & LASHLEY.

  SUNTAN LOTION,
  THE GIFT YOU WRAP AND THEN FORGET TO BRING.
  I WANNA MAN THAT STAYS TRUE, A DIAMOND RING TOO.
  DON'T SUGGEST NO SECOND BEST.
  I GOT A LOTTA LOVE TO BRING. I GOT A LOVE SONG TO
     SING.
  AND I'M NOT GONNA SETTLE FOR LESS THAN EVERYTHING.

    *(As the song ends, the crowd goes wild. In darkness,
    sound of a massive tour bus crashing.)*

Scene One

(Sparkley Clean Dry Cleaners.)

(The tail-end of the song **"THE HONKY WITHOUT THE TONKY"** *plays on the radio.* **JUNIE,** *the now ex-back-up singer for The Lashley Sisters, enters the family dry-cleaning business. She wears a neck brace.)*

DJ KYLE T. *(Voiceover.)* It's Monday, May 5th and you got Kyle T. tellin' it like it is from Ashland City, Tennessee. That last song was *The Honky without the Tonky* by *The Lashley Sisters.* Sad to say it, but I think those gals are gonna have to settle for a lot less than everything at this point. That's what happens when you drink and drive, Little Buddies.

*(**JUNIE** turns off the radio.)*

[MUSIC NO. 2 "BACK AT THE SPARKLEY"]

JUNIE.
BACK AT THE SPARKLEY DRY-CLEANIN' LIFE,
MOSTLY GETTIN' IT WRONG WHILE I TRY TO GET IT RIGHT.
WISHIN' ON A FALLIN' STAR THAT DOESN'T BURN AS
   BRIGHT,
OH LORD! I'M BACK AT THE SPARKLEY DRY-CLEANIN' LIFE!
GOOD MORNIN', COUNTER, HANGERS, STAPLER,

(Singing to a large picture of her mother.)

GOOD MORNIN', MAMA.
HERE'S TODAY'S READING FROM *STARTING OVER AFTER
FALLING APART*:

*(**JUNIE** reads from a book titled "Starting Over After Falling Apart.")*

NUMBER ONE: REMEMBER, ROCK BOTTOM MAKES AN
   AWESOME FLOOR.
NUMBER TWO: IF OPPORTUNITY DON'T KNOCK, YOU CAN
   ALWAYS BUILD A DOOR!

NUMBER THREE: ONE DAY AT A TIME IS THE BEST WAY TO
    START OVER.
OH, THAT REMINDS ME, KEEP MY SISTER CLEAN AND SOBER.
BACK AT THE SPARKLEY DRY-CLEANIN' BUSINESS,
CREASE THESE PANTS, SEW THE BUTTON, WHAT COLOR IS
    THIS?
GUESS I'LL CALL IT, HMMM, PURPLE POLYESTER OCHRE.
HOW'D MY LIFE GO FROM BEIN' GREAT TO MEDIOCRE?
WISHIN' ON A FALLIN' STAR THAT DOESN'T BURN AS
    BRIGHT,
OH LORD! I'M BACK AT THE SPARKLEY DRY, DRY, DRY-
    CLEANIN' LIFE.

    *(**PASTOR PHIL** enters with an armload of clothes.)*

PASTOR PHIL. Hey there, Junie.

JUNIE. Hey, Pastor Phil.

    *(**PASTOR PHIL** drops his shirts and goes in for a
    hug.)*

PASTOR PHIL. I am so glad you are still alive.

JUNIE. That makes two of us.

PASTOR PHIL. *(As he continues to hug **JUNIE**.)* No, I mean it. I
am so happy you are still in my life.

JUNIE. You are?

PASTOR PHIL. When I heard how y'all's tour bus jumped
the curb and flew through the air all catty-corner and
sideways, I thought to myself, I am so grateful my girl
Junie did not get squashed.

JUNIE. Thank you. It was a definite wake-up call; especially
since everybody but my sister Lashley was sound asleep
when it happened.

PASTOR PHIL. How's your injured neck? Can I do anything
for it?

JUNIE. No. Doctor Milo said I could stop wearing the neck
brace a good two weeks ago, but I just want to make
sure it's extra better before I take it off.

PASTOR PHIL. Here, let me say a silent healing prayer for it.

JUNIE. I've never heard of such a –

> *(He suddenly puts his hands on her neck.)*

Oh, okay.

PASTOR PHIL. *(Praying.)* Mmmhmmm, mmhmmm, Amen.

> *(Star-struck.)*

I still can't believe *The Lashley Sisters* are now the people starching my shirts and pressing my pants.

JUNIE. Don't be too impressed.

PASTOR PHIL. Seriously, y'all's song *Big Boned Dreams, Tiny Tambourines* is like an arrow to my heart every time I hear it.

JUNIE. Sounds dangerous.

PASTOR PHIL. So, you think you'll start singing again soon?

JUNIE. No, ever since the record label dropped us, my sister won't sing.

PASTOR PHIL. Why can't you just sing?

JUNIE. Oh no, I'm just the harmonizer. Lashley's the one who's the singer singer.

PASTOR PHIL. Don't you miss singing?

JUNIE. Of course, but no one wants to book us right now anyway, what with all our bad publicity and all.

PASTOR PHIL. I'll hire you.

JUNIE. You will?

PASTOR PHIL. Yeah. My funeral singer has done departed and I need someone to sing her funeral.

JUNIE. Bindy Moss died?

PASTOR PHIL. Yep, contracted a case of toxoplasmosis and just keeled over.

JUNIE. That's the way it is. One minute you're eating a flank steak, the next you got yourself an opportunistic infection. Poor Bindy... You know, she used to make me my own batch of snickerdoodles every Ashland City Summerfest.

PASTOR PHIL. So, you'll do it then?

JUNIE. I wish I could, but I gotta stop dreamin' and start dry cleanin'.

PASTOR PHIL. Look, life is too short to not go after the things you love with everything you got. I suppose you heard about the whole arsonist thing that's been going on?

JUNIE. Arsonist thing?

[MUSIC NO. 3 "DEATH IS EVERYWHERE"]

PASTOR PHIL.
THERE'S AN ARSONIST ON THE LOOSE NEAR WHITE
     BRIDGE ROAD.

JUNIE. Oh my!

PASTOR PHIL.
BURNT THREE DOG HOUSES, A CAMPER AND A DUPLEX
     HOME.
A DOG NAMED CARL IS THE SOLE SURVIVOR.
ONLY EVIDENCE IS A BUTANE LIGHTER.
THERE'S AN ARSONIST ON THE LOOSE NEAR WHITE BRIDGE
     ROAD.

JUNIE.
COULD BE A RUNAWAY TRAIN OR A TAINTED PEAR.

PASTOR PHIL.
YOU COULD COUGH TILL YOU DROP. DEATH IS
     EVERYWHERE!

JUNIE.
YOU COULD CHOKE ON LINT, SLIP ON BLACK ICE.

PASTOR PHIL.
WHEN YOU THINK ABOUT YOUR LIFE, YOU BEST THINK
     TWICE.

JUNIE & PASTOR PHIL.
YOU COULD DIE! IN THE BLINK OF AN EYE!

PASTOR PHIL.
DEATH IS EVERYWHERE.

JUNIE.
NINE PEOPLE HAD NO IDEA THEY'D DRAW THEIR LAST
     BREATH,

WHEN THEY UNBEKNOWNST PACKED A BROWN BAG LUNCH
OF DEATH.

IT'S A SAD, SAD THING YOU CAN'T FIGURE OR FACTOR

THAT YOUR LOVED ONE GOT KILLT BY A PEANUT BUTTER
CRACKER.

THEY UNBEKNOWNST PACKED A BROWN BAG LUNCH OF
DEATH.

COULD BE A LITTLE BITTY BUG OR A BIG BLACK BEAR.

PASTOR PHIL.

YOU COULD SMOKE TILL YOU CROAK!

JUNIE.

DEATH IS EVERYWHERE.

YOU COULD DROWN IN YOUR TUB, FREEZE IN SNOW.

PASTOR PHIL.

THE DAY OR THE HOUR DON'T NONE OF US KNOW.

JUNIE & PASTOR PHIL.

YOU COULD DIE! IN THE BLINK OF AN EYE!

JUNIE.

DEATH IS EVERYWHERE.

THE WHOLE WORLD'S TOPSY-TURVY

PASTOR PHIL.

EVER SINCE THE FALL OF MAN.

JUNIE & PASTOR PHIL.

THE WHOLE WORLD'S TOPSY-TURVY.

PASTOR PHIL.

YOU GOTTA TRUST IN THE GOOD LORD'S PLAN.

JUNIE & PASTOR PHIL.

THE WHOLE WORLD'S TOPSY-TURVY.

JUNIE.

ALL THIS TOTTERING ON THE BRINK!

JUNIE & PASTOR PHIL.

THE WHOLE WORLD'S TOPSY-TURVY.

PASTOR PHIL.

FEELS LIKE THIS SHIP'S ABOUT TO SINK.

JUNIE.

THAT'S WHY, WHEN YOU THINK ABOUT YOUR LIFE YOU
BEST THINK TWICE,

JUNIE & PASTOR PHIL.
> 'CAUSE DEATH IS EVERYWHERE.

PASTOR PHIL. All right then, the funeral is day after tomorrow.

JUNIE. Your shirts aren't gonna steam press themselves.

PASTOR PHIL. Look, y'all might be one dead person away from getting your next record deal.

JUNIE. I never thought of it like that. Tell you what, I'll run on home and get Lashley on board with this new casket singing-slash-career opportunity.

PASTOR PHIL. I'll call you if anybody else dies.

JUNIE. Sounds good. Well, not good, but...yeah.

> (**JUNIE** *and* **PASTOR PHIL** *exit in opposite directions.*)

Scene Two

(**LASHLEY** *family kitchen.*)

(*Mid-morning on the same day. Various appliances clutter the counter.* **LYLE LASHLEY** *sits at the kitchen table.* **LASHLEY LASHLEY** *looks at a bank statement as she talks on the phone. She wears a robe.*)

LASHLEY. *(On phone.)* Hey, Murray, it's Lashley. I was looking at our *Lashley Sisters* bank account and I'm wondering if there's some sort of mistake here. I know we had to pay off all the damages from the bus crash and all, but... Oh, a hundred and sixty-eight thousand is not so bad. Come again? As in, cents? One dollar and sixty-eight cents? Okay, thanks for letting me know.

(**LASHLEY** *hangs up.* **LYLE** *talks to his daughter as if she's a stranger.*)

LYLE. Young Lady, I would like to order a steak with a baked potato, please.

LASHLEY. How 'bout cereal instead?

(**LASHLEY** *gives him a bowl of cereal.*)

LYLE. My wife's on her way. She took a separate car this time.

LASHLEY. Well, she sure is taking a heckuva long time to get here.

LYLE. Our band just played a gig over in Memphis.

LASHLEY. Thirty-five years ago to be exact.

LYLE. We're *The Humming Humdingers.* Have you heard of us?

LASHLEY. Daddy, it's me.

(**LASHLEY** *puts a piece of bread into the toaster.*)

LYLE. Well, hello, Me. Nice to meet you.

LASHLEY. *(As she hugs him.)* No offense, Daddy, but this Alzheimer's thing of yours really blows.

LYLE. My wife's on her way. She took a separate car this time.

LASHLEY. Of all the memories for you to remember over and over, why in King's Carnation does it have to be the night Mama left us?

[MUSIC NO. 3B "VOCAL WARM UP"]

JUNIE. *(Offstage.) (Singing scales.)*
LA LA LA LA LA.

LYLE & JUNIE.
LA LA LA LA LA.

LASHLEY. Oh crap, Junie's back from the Sparkley. Let's just pretend I ain't home.

*(As **LASHLEY** goes to exit, **JUNIE** enters, still wearing the neck brace.)*

JUNIE. *(Singing.)*
GOOD AFTERNOON, LASHLEY. ME MAY MOO MOH MAH, GOOD, BE BO BE BO DAY, DEAR DADDY.

JUNIE & LYLE.
ME MAY MOO MOH MAH, GOOD, BE BO BE BO DAY, DEAR DADDY.

*(**LASHLEY** gets a tub of margarine out of the fridge.)*

JUNIE. You sound good, Daddy.

*(Taking margarine away from **LASHLEY**.)*

Oh, by the way, let's all make a pact to not eat any margarine anymore. I know you love it, but…

(Throwing margarine into trash.)

Did you know that margarine is something like one molecule away from being plastic? How is that possible? Isn't someone somewhere in charge of things that are supposedly edible? I mean, how can plastic particles even be digestible? And now, I find out, I'm one tiny molecule away from coating my spleen with Tupperware. That is not a comforting thought. No wonder there's cancer everywhere.

(LASHLEY retrieves the margarine as JUNIE puts various appliances away.)

LASHLEY. Don't put that stuff away. I'm havin' a sidewalk sale.

JUNIE. You can't sell this stuff, every single bit of it still works.

LASHLEY. We don't need two juicers, Junie.

JUNIE. All right, fine, you can sell one of the juicers.

(LASHLEY grabs one of the electric juicers.)

Not that one, this one.

(Handing LASHLEY a small manual, plastic citrus juicer.)

Why are you still goin' around in your robe? Do you not feel well or something?

LASHLEY. I don't know. What is it you want from me?

JUNIE. Do you think it might be strep? 'Cause we can't afford to get no strep right now. You might end up infecting the pastor.

You know how big he is on huggin' everybody.

LASHLEY. The pastor? What pastor?

JUNIE. Pastor Phil from that new church I been goin' to.

LASHLEY. Oh right, the guy you have a crush on.

JUNIE. I do not have a crush on Pastor Phil.

LASHLEY. Whatever you say, Junie.

JUNIE. And what I say is what I mean. The man is married, Lashley.

LYLE. Our band just played a gig over in Memphis. We're *The Humming Humdingers*. Ever heard of us?

[MUSIC NO. 3C "HUMDINGER A CAPELLA"]

JUNIE. I sure have.

HUMDINGER, HUMDINGER SING ALONG,

JUNIE & LYLE.

AIN'T NOTHIN' LIKE A CATAWAMPUS HUMDINGER SONG.

LASHLEY. Why does your pastor friend want to meet with us again?

JUNIE. Because, and you are gonna love this, he's gone and hired us to be his new funeral singers.

LASHLEY. Say what?

JUNIE. He heard how we lost our record deal. And he and I got to talking 'bout how hard it is to, you know, be an artist and all, especially you being an alcoholic artist. Anyway, long story short, looks like we're gonna be doing our act again, but with different lyrics.

LASHLEY. I am not gonna go around singing for a bunch of dead people.

JUNIE. I already told him we'd do it.

LASHLEY. Why can't you just funeral sing by yourself?

JUNIE. Because the deal is, you're the one sings lead and I'm the one sings harmony. That's why.

LASHLEY. Are you being serious with me?

JUNIE. Look, a lot of bigwig record producer-types know people that die on a regular basis.

LASHLEY. Exactly. I mean, come on, Junie. We sang live at the Grand Ole Opry. We can't go from that to this.

JUNIE. You can't give up just 'cause we've had a few setbacks.

LASHLEY. Setbacks? I did seven shots of Cuervo in the span of thirty minutes and then went and plowed our tour bus into a pet store. I literally killed puppies.

JUNIE. You didn't mean to –

LASHLEY. You can't come back as a country singer after you've gone and killed puppies.

JUNIE. Of course you can. Country music is built on drunken, jail-time-serving cheaters makin' their musical comeback.

LASHLEY. You sound exactly like Mama did. Why can't you just sing while you do the laundry and be satisfied?

[MUSIC NO. 4 "BIG TIME PLANS"]

JUNIE. Like Mama would ever be satisfied just singing while
she separated socks.

JUNIE.

WHEN I HEAR THE STARTER PISTOL, SISTER, I WANNA GO.
PUT ME ON A BULL AT THE RODEO.
I WANNA FEEL THE HOT SPOTLIGHT ON ME AT MY
    MICROPHONE
FRONT AND CENTER SINGING AT THE SUPER BOWL.

LASHLEY.

ARE YOU LISTENIN' TO ME? MY ANSWER IS NO.
LET ME BREAK IT DOWN FOR YOU, I'M ON A WHOLE OTHER
    TRACK.
YOU WANNA LIVE IN THE PAST, WELL, I AIN'T GOIN' BACK.
JUST THE THOUGHT OF IT MAKES ME WANNA DO A SHOT
    OF JACK.

JUNIE.

FUNERAL SINGIN'S SERIOUS BUSINESS, DON'T JOKE LIKE
    THAT!

LASHLEY.

THERE'S NO SINGIN' IN MY DREAMS.

JUNIE.

IS THAT A FACT?!

JUNIE & LASHLEY.

LOOK AT ME, YOU'LL SEE THAT I'M ON FIRE.
LOOK AT ME AND YOU'LL KNOW WHO I AM.
I'M POSITIVELY B-B-BURNING WITH AMBITION AND DESIRE.
I MAY BE A SMALL TOWN MAMA BUT I'VE GOT MYSELF SOME
    BIG TIME PLANS.

JUNIE.

YOU BE MY GEORGE JONES, I'LL BE YOUR TAMMY WYNETTE!

LASHLEY.

I'D RATHER BUY A LOTTO TICKET AND JUST SEE WHAT I
    CAN GET.

JUNIE.

BUT WE'RE A NATURAL BORN, SECOND TIME'S A CHARM,
    SISTER SINGIN' DUET.

LASHLEY.

DEAD PEOPLE DON'T INT'REST ME.

JUNIE.

BUT THEY'RE A SURE FIRE BET! EVERYBODY DIES!

JUNIE & LASHLEY.

LOOK AT ME, YOU'LL SEE THAT I'M ON FIRE.

LOOK AT ME AND YOU'LL KNOW WHO I AM.

I'M POSITIVELY B-B-BURNING WITH AMBITION AND DESIRE.

I MAY BE A SMALL TOWN MAMA BUT I'VE GOT MYSELF SOME BIG TIME PLANS.

I, I MAY BE A SMALL TOWN MAMA BUT I'VE GOT MYSELF SOME BIG TIME PLANS.

I MAY BE A SMALL TOWN MAMA BUT I'VE GOT MYSELF SOME BIG TIME PLANS.

LASHLEY. Sorry, Junie, music is no longer my thing.

JUNIE. Did I or did I not put my whole life on hold while I travelled across the entire map of the United States being a back-up singer for you?

LASHLEY. I guess you did, but –

JUNIE. Not to mention the fact, I've been Daddy's number one caretaker while you were gallivanting God knows where, participating in all your drinking straight tequila parties.

LASHLEY. Guilt me all you want, but from now on, my vocal cords are off-limits.

JUNIE. Okay, fine. I'll tell Pastor Phil someone else will have to sing poor Bindy off to her eternal home.

LASHLEY. Yes, you will.

> (*As* **JUNIE** *puts the rest of the appliances away, she notices/reads the bank statement.*)

> **[*MUSIC NO. 4B "HUMDINGER A CAPPELLA"*]**

LYLE.

GLAD TO SEE YOU, GLAD TO SEE YOU,

GLAD TO SEE YOU WHEN YOU COME HOME.

JUNIE. All we have left in our *Lashley Sisters* account is a dollar and sixty-eight cents?

LASHLEY. I know it's a shock, but –

JUNIE. I'll tell you what's a shock, the fact you won't sing a few funerals, especially since you almost went and broke my one and only neck.

LASHLEY. Okay, yes, I'll do it.

JUNIE. *The Lashley Sisters* are back! You'll see, now that you're sober, you are gonna love singing in a whole new deep down way.

LASHLEY. You do realize I do my best singing when I'm totally tanked, right?

JUNIE. We are gonna be soothing folks in the first flush of the grieving process. So, you gotta stick to your twelve steps full-time now. Anyhoo, I'm gonna go do some research see what all casket singing entails.

> (**JUNIE** *exits.* **LASHLEY** *pulls out an unopened bottle of bourbon.*)

LASHLEY. I still think she should just burial sing by herself.

LYLE. *(Suddenly lucid.)* Your sister's not the lead singer type, you are.

LASHLEY. Daddy, are you you?

LYLE. I was the last time I checked.

> *(Realizing that her dad, in this moment, knows who she is,* **LASHLEY** *hugs her dad.)*

LASHLEY. Hey, Daddy! It's good to see you.

LYLE. Hey, Peanut.

LASHLEY. Want more milk for your cereal?

LYLE. No. It's all right. I always thought that you and your sister were like a fish and a bird; two totally different species.

LASHLEY. I must be the fish then 'cause my life is definitely under water.

LYLE. Some people spend their whole lives being something they're not. That never happens in nature. You'd never see a zebra acting like a centipede or a cow trying to be some monkey.

LASHLEY. That's true.

LYLE. You were born to fly, Lashley. Because you, my dear, are a beautiful little bird.

> (**LYLE** *touches the bottle of bourbon.*)

Don't stay under water too long, Peanut.

LASHLEY. I won't, Daddy.

> (*Strengthened by her dad,* **LASHLEY** *puts the unopened bottle of bourbon away.*)

Scene Three

(Third United Separated Harmony Church.)

(Bindy Moss funeral.)

(PASTOR PHIL *preaches.* **JUNIE, LASHLEY,** *and* **LYLE** *sit nearby.* **JUNIE** *wears an aquamarine dress.)*

PASTOR PHIL. Without a vision, the people perish. I'm sure you will all agree when I say, Bindy Moss had vision. Amen?

JUNIE. Amen!

PASTOR PHIL. It was Bindy who started our church hugging circle. Bindy who got us all going fat-free for the Father. I think we lost a cumulative fifty pounds on that one. Bindy Moss was not an onlooker. She was a looker. She had an eagle eye for the misfit, the lonely and the off-kilter soul. Why just last month, I was going through a spiritual sag, of sorts. Out of the blue, here comes Bindy with a just-out-of-the oven coffee cake. I said, Bindy, ever since my wife Midge packed up everything she owned and left me, I've lost track of it all. And now here I am just plumb full of doubt. Without missin' a beat she says, "Sounds to me like your dream truck's gone and got four flat tires, Pastor Phil. You got to come up with some new doable dreams." Well, don't you know, I got out my "to-do" list and put down "come up with a doable dream." And even though my wife has yet to return any of my phone calls, I haven't had a slump since. I have, however, had a heck of a lot of coffee cake.

(Looking heavenward.)

Thank you, Bindy, you helped me part-way through a rough, hard time.

(To Congregation and The Lashley Sisters.)

And now, it is my great honor and privilege to introduce *The Lashley Sisters.* I still can't believe two of the most talented, nominally famous country singers are gonna be singing funerals for us. I have been a fan of y'all's music ever since your first single, *Seven Times Ago,* came out. I especially loved the lyric, "And we danced back into forgiveness. As she whispered, I mean it this time." Matter of fact, I played that song on my wife's voicemail just last night.

LASHLEY. The whole song?

PASTOR PHIL. Every single note.

JUNIE. Thank you, Pastor Phil. And let me just say, Lashley and I are both extremely excited about being here at Third United Separated Harmony Church.

LASHLEY. Oh yeah, ever since you hired us, we've been making lists of all the death-type songs we could sing.

JUNIE. But today, we want to celebrate the life of Bindy Moss. Focus on the details her family might want to hear about most in their sad time of loss.

> (**LASHLEY** *holds up a shirt.*)

> **[MUSIC NO. 5 "BINDY TAKE A SEAT AT THE BANQUET TABLE ('CAUSE THERE'S NO NEED FOR FOOD DRIVES IN HEAVEN)"]**

LASHLEY.

> YESTERDAY, I CAME ACROSS BINDY'S FAVORITE FOOD DRIVE SHIRT.

JUNIE. She brought it in to the Sparkley to be dry-cleaned last Tuesday.

LASHLEY. Oh good, that grape juice stain from her grandson came out.

JUNIE.

> I THINK SHE WORE THIS SHIRT FOR EVERY CHURCH FOOD DRIVE SHE WORKED.

LASHLEY. Lord, that woman sure did work a lot of food drives.

JUNIE. That woman got more businesses to donate canned goods than anyone else I know from here to Coffee County.

LASHLEY.

YEP, BINDY MOSS WAS SOMEONE MADE THE

LASHLEY & JUNIE.

MOST OF HER TIME,

DURING HER SHORT TIME HERE ON EARTH!

LASHLEY.

BINDY,

JUNIE.

BINDY,

LASHLEY & JUNIE.

BINDY, TAKE A SEAT!

JUNIE.

TAKE A LOAD OFF!

LASHLEY & JUNIE.

YOU BEEN WORKIN' FOR THE LORD SINCE YOU WERE
     SEVEN.

TAKE A SEAT NOW, BINDY, AT THE BANQUET TABLE,

'CAUSE THERE'S NO NEED FOR FOOD DRIVES IN HEAVEN.

LASHLEY.

SHE WAS A UNIFIER,

JUNIE.

AN AVID BIRD FEEDER,

LASHLEY.

A

LASHLEY & JUNIE

GIVER WITH A CAPITAL GIVE.

JUNIE.

BINDY MOSS WAS A FOURTH GRADE TEACHER,

HER LIFE A LESSON ON HOW TO LIVE.

LASHLEY.

SHE WAS A BIG RECYCLER,

JUNIE.

A ROCK COLLECTOR,

LASHLEY & JUNIE.

TAUGHT SWIMMING AT THE YMCA.

LASHLEY.

A FOOD DRIVE MAVEN,

JUNIE.

A PEOPLE CONNECTOR,

LASHLEY.

HAD TWO KIDNEYS, BUT SHE GAVE ONE AWAY.

BINDY,

JUNIE.

BINDY,

LASHLEY & JUNIE.

BINDY, TAKE A SEAT!

JUNIE.

TAKE A LOAD OFF!

LASHLEY & JUNIE.

YOU'VE BEEN WORKIN' FOR THE LORD SINCE YOU WERE
　　SEVEN.

TAKE A SEAT NOW, BINDY, AT THE BANQUET TABLE,

'CAUSE THERE'S NO NEED FOR FOOD DRIVES IN HEAVEN.

PULL UP A CHAIR AND LAY YOUR BURDEN,

PULL UP A CHAIR AND LAY YOUR BURDEN DOWN, DOWN,
　　DOWN.

BINDY,

BINDY,

BINDY, TAKE A SEAT!

JUNIE.

EVERYBODY NOW!

LASHLEY, JUNIE & PASTOR PHIL.

YOU'VE BEEN WORKIN' FOR THE LORD SINCE YOU WERE
　　SEVEN.

TAKE A SEAT NOW, BINDY, AT THE BANQUET TABLE.

'CAUSE THERE'S NO NEED FOR FOOD DRIVES IN HEAVEN.

THE LORD DON'T NEED NO FOOD DRIVES IN HEAVEN.

LASHLEY. By the way, if any of you need to take your mind off your grief, I'll be having a sidewalk sale day after tomorrow from twelve to five.

JUNIE. We all have Bindy on our minds and in our hearts. That's what my sister Lashley meant most of all.

PASTOR PHIL. *(Praying.)* Lord, we thank you for the life of Bindy.

LYLE. *(To* **PASTOR PHIL.***)* Your suit is very noisy.

JUNIE. Daddy, we're praying.

PASTOR PHIL. Uuuh… Lord, we ask for your guidance, comfort and –

LYLE. Every time you move, it sounds like a newspaper opening up.

PASTOR PHIL. Uh, amen. Blessings to you all. Now go in peace over to the fellowship hall for fruit, beverages and some of Wanda Lynn's Meat and Egg Jell-O Salad.

LYLE. *(He raises* **PASTOR PHIL***'s arm.)* Hear that? Sounds like a brown paper bag every time you move.

> *(***LYLE** *takes* **PASTOR PHIL***'s jacket.)*

LASHLEY. Daddy, we're not at the dry cleaners right now.

LYLE. Sorry, Miss, but this man was here first. How about Tuesday?

PASTOR PHIL. Tuesday works.

LYLE. Now, what can I do for you, Young Lady?

> *(Forgetting her purse,* **LASHLEY** *leads* **LYLE** *toward the fellowship hall.)*

LASHLEY. I have an emergency.

LYLE. Oh!

LASHLEY. It's called lunch.

> *(***LASHLEY** *and* **LYLE** *exit.)*

JUNIE. I really enjoyed the doable dream part of your eulogy, Pastor Phil.

PASTOR PHIL. Thank you, Junie. You look very pretty today.

JUNIE. Thank you! People always have said that aquamarine is my color.

PASTOR PHIL. Oh, it is.

JUNIE. Okay, well, I'm gonna go and make myself a plate of Wanda Lynn's Meat and Egg Jell-O. You want some?

PASTOR PHIL. Absotootinlootly!

(JUNIE *exits.* **PASTOR PHIL** *calls his estranged wife.*)

Hey, Midge, it's me. I know you said you didn't want to speak. But you've been silent so long, I'm wonderin' did you mean forever? As in never? Anyway, I was just hoping you might answer.

(*Dejected,* **PASTOR PHIL** *hangs up. He compulsively pulls out/looks at a Daily Race Form.* **PASTOR PHIL** *looks around and then makes another call.*)

Hey, Bobby. How's Big Dream lookin' for the third race?

(*Unseen and in search of her purse,* **LASHLEY** *re-enters.*)

No, just put me in for Big Dream in the third. No, that's all. I just want a taste.

(**PASTOR PHIL** *hangs up.*)

LASHLEY. Big Dream in the third, huh?

PASTOR PHIL. I have a little bit of a gambling issue.

LASHLEY. How little is it?

PASTOR PHIL. I'm on the verge of losing my house and my wife's left me.

LASHLEY. Would it make you feel better if I told you I've been divorced three times and I drank away every cent I ever made?

PASTOR PHIL. Not better, but less alone. Congratulations for making it through your rehab, by the way.

LASHLEY. Evidently, I am now one hundred percent rehabilitated.

PASTOR PHIL. I wish I could say that.

[MUSIC NO. 6 "NO IMPULSE CONTROL"]

LASHLEY. Believe me, when I say, I'm not sayin' all that much, 'cause…

> *(Singing.)*

> I GOT NO IMPULSE CONTROL.
> LISTEN. I LIKE TO DRINK. I LIKE TO PARTY.
> AIN'T NO BIG THING, IT'S JUST A GOOD TIME.
> SO, WHY FIGHT IT? I'M AN ALCHY,
> ADDICTED TO TEQUILA AND LIME.
> I GOT NO IMPULSE CONTROL. NO IMPULSE CONTROL.
> ONCE I WENT OUT FOR PANCAKES, WOUND UP EATING KOREAN,
> WOKE UP ON A PLANE BOUND FOR SEOUL. I GOT NO IMPULSE CONTROL.

> *(Talking.)*

> Sound familiar?

PASTOR PHIL.

> I LIKE TO PICK 'EM. I LIKE THE TICKET.
> I LIKE IT BEST WHEN I BEAT THE HOUSE.
> I PUT A FAVORITE WITH A LONG SHOT.
> SEE, THAT'S THE BEST WAY TO LOSE A SPOUSE.
> I GOT NO IMPULSE CONTROL.
> NO IMPULSE CONTROL.
> ONCE I LOST A HALF MIL THE SAME NIGHT I WAS WILLED IT,
> AND WHAT'S WORSE MY WIFE DIDN'T EVEN KNOW.
> I GOT

LASHLEY & PASTOR PHIL.

> NO IMPULSE CONTROL.

LASHLEY. If I could just take the first step of those twelve steps.

PASTOR PHIL. Yeah, if you didn't have to take that first step, the other eleven would be easy…

LASHLEY.

> AFTER THE THIRD DRINK, THE REAL ME ARRIVES.

PASTOR PHIL.

WHEN I PLACE A BET, I'M A HAPPIER GUY.

LASHLEY & PASTOR PHIL.

WHEN I'M EMPTY INSIDE, I WANNA GET ON THAT RIDE.

AND SINCE I'M ALWAYS EMPTY, I'M ALWAYS CHASIN' THAT HIGH.

I GOT NO IMPULSE CONTROL. NO IMPULSE CONTROL.

LASHLEY.

ONCE I WOKE UP IN TUCSON WITH A HANGOVER AND A RING ON.

PASTOR PHIL.

IF MY HORSES RAN FASTER, I'D BE A MORE PEACEFUL PASTOR.

LASHLEY & PASTOR PHIL.

SOMEDAY WE'LL KICK IT. SOMEDAY WE'LL QUIT.

IN THE MEANTIME, WE'LL EACH PLAY OUR ROLE

> *(Unseen,* **JUNIE** *enters with a plate of food for* **PASTOR PHIL.***)*

LASHLEY.

OF

LASHLEY & PASTOR PHIL.

NO IMPULSE CONTROL. NO IMPULSE CONTROL. NO IMPULSE –

> *(***JUNIE** *watches as* **PASTOR PHIL** *suddenly kisses* **LASHLEY.** **JUNIE** *coughs.)*

LASHLEY. You okay there, Junie?

JUNIE. *(To* **LASHLEY.***)* Are you okay?

> *(To* **PASTOR PHIL.***)*

Here, Pastor Phil, I made you a plate of food.

PASTOR PHIL. Thank you.

JUNIE. Well, you know, we should all take care to take care of the people we care about. Especially since, we have no idea how long they will be around for us to care about them.

LASHLEY. Say what?

JUNIE. While scooping out some extra radishes for your plate, I learned that a man and his dog have died. So, if you two lovey-birds will excuse me, I'm going to go write a song with the working title *Resting in Larger Arms than Mine.*

(JUNIE *exits.*)

PASTOR PHIL. I guess I should go and find out –

LASHLEY. Which dog died?

PASTOR PHIL. Chances are, it's gonna be a shared coffin funeral.

(PASTOR PHIL *exits.*)

Scene Four

(Sparkley Clean Dry Cleaners.)

(Unopened boxes clutter the dry cleaners. **LYLE** *has found a picture of his wife inside one of the smaller boxes. He talks to his wife's picture.)*

LYLE. *(To picture.)* I wrote this song for you on our third date, remember, Maddy?

[MUSIC NO. 7 "SWEET MACAROON"]

STRAWBERRIES, WARM MAPLE SYRUP,
APPLES PICKED RIGHT OFF THE TREE.

*(***LASHLEY*** *enters with a large box.)*

NOTHING COMPARES TO YOUR LOVE, MY DEAR.

*(***JUNIE*** *frantically rushes in, looking for her dad.)*

JUNIE. Lashley, have you seen Daddy?

(Relieved to see her father, **JUNIE** *listens to* **LYLE** *sing.)*

LYLE.
YOUR SMILE IS LIKE SUNSHINE TO ME.
YOU'RE MY SWEET

LYLE & LASHLEY.
MACAROON,

LYLE.
MY SWEET

LYLE & LASHLEY.
MACAROON,

*(***JUNIE*** *sings along with her dad and sister.)*

LYLE, JUNIE & LASHLEY.
MEET ME TONIGHT 'NEATH THE MOON, MY MACAROON.

LYLE.
YOU'RE MY

LYLE, JUNIE & LASHLEY.
SWEET MACAROON,

LYLE.
>
> MY

LYLE, JUNIE & LASHLEY.
>
> SWEET MACAROON,
>
> MEET ME TONIGHT 'NEATH THE MOON, MY MACAROON.

> *(LASHLEY notices LYLE's box.)*

LASHLEY. Oooo, what's in this box?

LYLE. *(Happily holding the box.)* My box.

LASHLEY. I just want to peek inside it, okay?

LYLE. *(Holding the box.)* Nope. Mine.

LASHLEY. *(Trying to take the box.)* Daddy –

JUNIE. He's so happy. Let him have it.

> *(LASHLEY relinquishes the box. LYLE happily escapes/exits with his box.)*

LYLE. *(Singing.)*

> YOU CAN WALK OUT THE DOOR, COME RIGHT BACK.
>
> I'LL BE GLAD TO SEE YOU WHEN YOU COME HOME.

> *(JUNIE looks at all of the boxes.)*

JUNIE. What is all this stuff anyway?

LASHLEY. These are articles of perfectly good dry cleaned clothes that folks never came to claim. So, I'm going to sell them at my upcoming sidewalk sale.

JUNIE. You and Pastor Phil sure did hit it off. He comin' to your sidewalk sale?

LASHLEY. *(Referring to her kiss with PASTOR PHIL.)* It was a mistake. Don't make a big deal of it.

> *(LASHLEY pulls a sweater out of a box. JUNIE takes the sweater.)*

JUNIE. I remember this sweater.

LASHLEY. *(Looking at the sweater.)* Daddy must've brought it over here after she left us.

JUNIE. *(Smelling the sweater.)* It smells like Mama.

LASHLEY. You just want it to.

JUNIE. It's her perfume, hyacinth, definitely.

(**JUNIE** *pulls a hat and dress out of the box.*)

Look, here's her yard work hat and her special occasion dress.

(**LASHLEY** *pulls a robe out of the box.*)

LASHLEY. And this was her, I'm-reading-all-day-leave-me-alone-robe.

(**JUNIE** *puts on the robe.*)

JUNIE. I loved it when the four of us piled into the Winnebago and headed off to sing at some festival or other.

LASHLEY. For your information, the family singing thing was a last-ditch effort 'cause Daddy was always trying to keep her from leaving us all like she never knew us to begin with.

JUNIE. What is wrong with you? You got a whole different Mama jammed up in your head. I loved her in this robe.

(**JUNIE** *finds a piece of paper in the robe pocket. She reads what's written on it to* **LASHLEY.**)

A poem for my daughters.

LASHLEY. What's it say?

JUNIE. Nothing. It's just the title.

LASHLEY. Sounds about right, more silence.

JUNIE. That's not the point. The point is it's proof she wanted to write us a poem, a tribute, a flush of motherly love is crammed into that title.

(**LASHLEY** *sees something in the box and acts excited.*)

LASHLEY. Look!

(*Hoping it's something wonderful,* **JUNIE** *moves closer.* **LASHLEY** *pulls out some old candy.*)

Some old peppermints!

(**JUNIE** *gives* **LASHLEY** *a look.*)

What? Least we know she had fresh breath.

JUNIE. I bet the rest of that poem is in here somewhere. In my heart of hearts, I truly believe Mama is coming back someday.

LASHLEY. Does it feel good, being full of all that unfounded hope?

JUNIE. Mama wouldn't just leave. She was plumb full of love.

(JUNIE *goes back to looking in the box.*)

LASHLEY. Yeah, I guess that's why she went off to find stardom all by herself.

JUNIE. Look, Mama and Daddy's old set list. Remember this one,

[MUSIC NO. 7A "BUG UP HER BUTT"]

SHE-EE HAD A BUG UP HER BUTT. SHE HAD A FROG IN HER THROAT.
SHE WAS A CROSS BETWEEN A BADGER AND A BILLY GOA –
TAH!

Or how about...

[MUSIC NO. 8 "LOVE HANGS ON"]

JUNIE.
THE LAST STRAW FELL 'BOUT A WEEK AGO.

Come on...

THAT CAMEL'S BACK HAS LONG BEEN BROKE.

I know you wanna sing it...

HAD THE PEDAL TO THE METAL TILL THE ENGINE BLEW.

LASHLEY. *(Joining in.)*
IT'S BEEN NON-STOP HARD FOR ME AND YOU.

LASHLEY & JUNIE.
DON'T YOU WORRY, BABY,
JUST HOLD ME TIGHT WHEN YOU DON'T FEEL STRONG.
DON'T YOU WORRY, BABY,
'CAUSE WHEN ALL SIGN OF HOPE IS GONE,
LOVE HANGS ON. LOVE HANGS ON.

LASHLEY.
> I CAN FEEL THE HARD TIMES CHANGING ME.
> I DON'T KNOW WHO I AM OR WHO I'LL BE.

JUNIE.
> DON'T YOU THINK THE SORROW MAKES US STRONG?
> DON'T YOU THINK THE NIGHT CAN'T LAST MUCH LONGER?

LASHLEY & JUNIE.
> DON'T YOU WORRY, BABY,
> JUST HOLD ME TIGHT WHEN YOU DON'T FEEL STRONG.
> DON'T YOU WORRY, BABY, 'CAUSE WHEN ALL SIGN OF HOPE
>   IS GONE,
> WHEN ALL SIGN OF HOPE IS GONE, WHEN ALL SIGN OF
>   HOPE IS GONE,
> LOVE HANGS ON.

> *(Sound of* **LYLE** *approaching.)*

LASHLEY. Take off Mama's robe. Daddy's coming.

JUNIE. I don't want to take it off.

LASHLEY. Take it off. You're going to upset him.

> *(***LYLE*** *enters.)*

JUNIE. Hey, Daddy.

> *(***JUNIE*** *holds up her mom's dress.)*

Look what I found!

LYLE. I know you.

JUNIE. It's Mama's smell.

LYLE. Is she coming now?

JUNIE. Smell it.

> *(***LYLE*** *takes the dress.)*

LASHLEY. No, Mama left us, Daddy.

> *(As* **JUNIE** *and* **LASHLEY** *argue,* **LYLE** *puts on his*
> *wife's dress.)*

JUNIE. Don't tell him that.

LASHLEY. Why not? It's the truth.

JUNIE. What good does it do him?

LASHLEY. The more we remind him of reality, the more he'll remember who we are.

JUNIE. Or, we can just enter into his reality.

LASHLEY. Like this?

> (**LASHLEY** *points to* **LYLE**, *who is now wearing the dress.*)

Here, Daddy, give me back Mama's dress, okay?

LYLE. No! Stay away from me.

LASHLEY. Daddy, I'm not trying to hurt you.

LYLE. Aaaauugh! Leave me alone, leave me alone!

> (*Unable to find/say the word he wants.*)

Patchwork! Patchwork!

> (*Hoping to calm him down,* **JUNIE** *sings to her dad.*)

[MUSIC NO. 9 "HUMDINGER SING ALONG"]

JUNIE.
HUMDINGER, HUMDINGER SING ALONG.
AIN'T NOTHIN' LIKE A CATAWAMPUS HUMDINGER SONG.
    HUM.
HOUSEFLIES HUM IN THE KEY OF F
'CEPTIN' ONE LITTLE FLY WHO WAS PLUMB TONE DEAF.

JUNIE & LYLE.
THAT LITTLE GUY...

LYLE.
HUMMED IN B FLAT
TO THE SUPERSONIC SOUNDS OF A MOUSE NAMED MATT.

JUNIE & LYLE.
THEY KEPT TIME WITH A DOG NAMED GAYLE
'CAUSE SHE KEPT A GOOD BEAT WHEN SHE WAGGED HER
    TAIL.

JUNIE.
IT WENT

JUNIE & LYLE.
GLAD TO SEE YOU, GLAD TO SEE YOU,

GLAD TO SEE YOU WHEN YOU COME HOME.
YOU CAN WALK OUT THE DOOR, COME RIGHT BACK,
I'LL BE GLAD TO SEE YOU WHEN YOU COME HO-HME.
HUMDINGER, HUMDINGER SING ALONG.
AIN'T NOTHIN' LIKE A CATAWAMPUS HUMDINGER SONG.

LYLE.

HUMAN BEINGS TRY TO PLAY IT COOL.

JUNIE.

DON'T WANNA BE FOUND LOOKIN' LIKE A FOOL.

LASHLEY.

WE COULD LEARN A THING OR TWO FROM OUR CANINE

JUNIE, LYLE & LASHLEY.

PUPS,

JUNIE & LASHLEY.

WHO NEVER TRY TO HIDE WHAT THEY

JUNIE, LYLE & LASHLEY.

FEEL FOR US.

LASHLEY.

SAYIN'

JUNIE, LASHLEY & LYLE.

GLAD TO SEE YOU, GLAD TO SEE YOU,
GLAD TO SEE YOU WHEN YOU COME HOME.

JUNIE & LASHLEY.

YOU CAN

JUNIE, LASHLEY & LYLE.

WALK OUT THE DOOR, COME RIGHT BACK,
I'LL BE GLAD TO SEE YOU WHEN YOU COME HOME.
GLAD TO SEE YOU, GLAD TO SEE YOU,
GLAD TO SEE YOU WHEN YOU COME HO-HME.

Scene Five

(Third United Separated Harmony Church.)

(Jimmy Boy Brown funeral.)

(PASTOR PHIL *preaches.* **JUNIE, LASHLEY** *and* **LYLE** *sit nearby.)*

PASTOR PHIL. There's so much that could be said about Jimmy Boy Brown. He won the Putnam County Tater Tot Eating Contest…once. His favorite color was taupe. He collected water heaters. But he was best known for the phrase, "Gratitude, the best thing for your attitude." As I prepared today's eulogy, I was listening to my *Lashley Sisters: Tribute to Historical Figures Live* album.

(Bursting into song.)

[MUSIC NO. 9B "TRIBUTE TO HISTORICAL FIGURES: LIVE"]

HARRY TRUMAN. ELEANOR ROOSEVELT. BAH DOOT DOOT BAH DOOT DOOT PSH! ROSA PARK-SAH!

(Mimicking drum sounds.)

What a great album! Now, Jimmy Boy wasn't famous or historical, but he did change my personal history when he single-handedly paid for my entire on-line seminary course.

(Looking heavenward.)

You were a light on the planet, Jimmy Boy, a light on the planet.

(JUNIE *puts some dog ears on her head and then barks like a dog.)*

[MUSIC NO. 10 "JIMMY BOY BROWN AND HIS TOY POODLE, PUDDIN'"]

JUNIE.

RUF RUF, RUF RUF, ROOOOO. RUF RUF, RUF RUF, ROOOOO.

LASHLEY.

JIMMY BOY BROWN AND HIS TOY POODLE PUDDIN' WERE
THE BESTEST OF THE BEST OF FRIENDS.

JUNIE.

THEY HAD A BROMANCE.

LASHLEY.

ONE WAS SWEETER THAN A PIE, ONE WAS CUTER THAN A
BUG,

JUNIE.

A LITTLE TINY BUG.

LASHLEY.

ONE MADE A MEAN JAMBALAYA,
ONE

JUNIE & LASHLEY.

PEED ON THE RUG,

JUNIE.

THE SHAGGY, SHAGGY RUG.

LASHLEY.

JIMMY LOVED HIS CAKE, BUT HE LOVED HIS PUDDIN' MORE.

JUNIE.

PUDDIN' LOVED THE SOUND OF AN

JUNIE & LASHLEY.

OLD RED FORD.
THEY WERE INSEPARABLE, BUT THE END WAS
UNAVOIDABLE.
THEIR LOVE WAS UNDENIABLE, BUT TIME HAS A WAY OF
STOPPIN' NOW
AND THEN.

JUNIE	**LASHLEY.**
AH-ROOO. AH-ROOO.	IT WAS A HOT SUMMER DAY WHEN
	A SOUND CAME A RATT'LIN'!
AH-ROOO. AH-ROOO.	PUDDIN' WAS GONE BEFORE JIMMY BOY COULD GRAB HIM.

JUNIE & LASHLEY.
> PUDDIN' CHASED THE CAR, JIMMY CHASED HIS DOG,
> BOTH DIED TOGETHER IN A DIRT ROAD FOG.
> THEY WERE INSEPARABLE, BUT THE END WAS
> > UNAVOIDABLE.
> THEIR LOVE WAS UNDENIABLE, BUT TIME HAS A WAY OF
> > STOPPIN' NOW
> AND THEN.

LASHLEY.
> BFFS, SIDEKICKS, HOME SKILLETS, BROS.

JUNIE.
> KEMO SABE LOVE STORY, INTER-SPECIES AMIGOS.

Scene Six

(**LASHLEY** *family kitchen.*)

(**JUNIE** *sits at the kitchen table looking through a box. She pulls out/reads two pieces of paper. She reads a third torn scrap of paper, then weeps.* **PASTOR PHIL** *knocks.*)

JUNIE. Yes.

(**PASTOR PHIL** *knocks.*)

I said, yes. Yes!

(**PASTOR PHIL** *enters.* **JUNIE** *weeps.*)

PASTOR PHIL. Oh. Bad time? This is a bad time?

JUNIE. No, I'm fine. What do you need?

PASTOR PHIL. I came to tell you that somebody died.

(**JUNIE** *wails.*)

Did you know them?

JUNIE. What?

PASTOR PHIL. It was a sudden sort of thing sort of and –

JUNIE. Who died?

PASTOR PHIL. The funeral is on Saturday.

JUNIE. Who's gone?

PASTOR PHIL. Arthur Reid.

JUNIE. Perfect.

PASTOR PHIL. Did you know him?

JUNIE. Kinda. We dated in Junior High. He said I had nice lips.

PASTOR PHIL. What?

JUNIE. Nice lips. He liked my lips.

PASTOR PHIL. Well, I can see that.

JUNIE. No, they're terrible.

(**PASTOR PHIL** *leans in to comfort her.*)

PASTOR PHIL. No really, I can see.

JUNIE. Really?

PASTOR PHIL. *(Leaning in again.)* Of course.

   *(*JUNIE *goes to kiss* **PASTOR PHIL.** *He pulls away.)*

I'm sorry. I meant to look at. Nice lips to look at.

JUNIE. But not kiss?

PASTOR PHIL. I'm married.

JUNIE. Except when it comes to my sister.

PASTOR PHIL. Junie.

JUNIE. No really, whatever. I don't want to kiss you anyway. I just want to be kissed someday, somehow, somewhere by somebody who feels something, some tiny little bit of everything for me.

Besides, I like Midge. Please don't tell her you almost kissed me.

PASTOR PHIL. What? No, I would never tell her that.

JUNIE. Because you're the one who leaned in. You may have pulled back, but before that part, you definitely leaned in.

PASTOR PHIL. I don't remember leaning in at all.

JUNIE. The body does what the body does.

PASTOR PHIL. What does that even mean?

JUNIE. We're adults. You know what it means and I know what it means. And you may think it means something different to you than it does to me, but the truth is, you meant it.

PASTOR PHIL. I didn't mean it at all.

JUNIE. Then what did you mean?

PASTOR PHIL. To comfort you?

JUNIE. Well, you have done the exact opposite. What kind of pastor are you?

PASTOR PHIL. A bad one?

JUNIE. I'll say.

  (Pause.)

I found my mama's papers.

(Holding up a piece of paper.)

She wrote about us. See? *A Poem for My Daughters.* That's the title. Well, I thought it was the title. It's really just a line in the middle of a stupid to-do list. See, I found the other half of the page.

(Holding up the scrap of paper.)

"Someday, maybe I'll write…

(Piecing two scraps of paper together.)

a poem for my daughters."

PASTOR PHIL. No poem then, huh?

JUNIE. No, at least not yet. All her writing's pretty mundane.

(Reading the other pieces of paper.)

"This haircut works." "Remember to buy blackberry jam for Lashley."

PASTOR PHIL. Why were you looking?

JUNIE. I wanted her advice. I have no idea how to get the life I want. I've been reading these self-help books. I've been praying. I've been working hard for years, and none of the things on my list are realities. Be a famous singer. No. Get married. No. Be financially stable. I don't even know what that means anymore.

PASTOR PHIL. I feel like this is all my fault. I know it was a bad example, my borderline infidelity with your sister.

JUNIE. My foundation has had hairline cracks in it for forever.

PASTOR PHIL. You're a good funeral singer. So much so, I'm thinking we should do weddings too.

JUNIE. Watching other people marry? That sounds very depressing to me.

PASTOR PHIL. It's not perfect, I know. But, maybe you'll meet someone soon.

(Leaning toward **JUNIE.***)*

I'm kinda shocked you're single.

JUNIE. Are you going to try and kiss me again?

(**LASHLEY** *enters with a wad of cash.*)

LASHLEY. That was the best sidewalk sale ever.

JUNIE. What'd you do sell everything for twice what it's worth? You better not have sold any of Mama's stuff.

LASHLEY. How could I? You carried it all into your bedroom. This is from the unclaimed dry-cleaning, which did include three fur coats. I don't know where I'm going yet, but I am gonna take me a real vacation somewhere.

JUNIE. Go for it. Travel round the world non-frickin-stop.

LASHLEY. What's the matter? You look like you been crying.

JUNIE. Arthur Reid died.

LASHLEY. Really?

JUNIE. That's what they say.

LASHLEY. Well, he was an odd duck, that's for sure.

JUNIE. No, he wasn't. He was a do-gooder. He built that naked people statue. He opened the Ashland City Archive Library.

LASHLEY. The what?

JUNIE. He started the Earth-centric Awareness Foundation.

LASHLEY. How did he die?

PASTOR PHIL. Choked on a corn bread chunk.

LASHLEY. Note to self. Even corn bread chunks need to be chewed.

JUNIE. You can joke all you want, but his life mattered, Lashley. He made his time here on Planet Earth really count.

LASHLEY. Okay.

JUNIE. A lot, a whole lot of people found him incredibly inspiring.

LASHLEY. Didn't Arthur Reid take you to your Middle School Graduation Dance?

JUNIE. That has nothing whatsoever to do with my high admiration for the man. He was a real go-getter –

LASHLEY. A do-gooder and a go-getter –

JUNIE. An energizer. He was wonderful.

LASHLEY. He did compliment my lips once.

JUNIE. What? When?

LASHLEY. I don't remember the details of the compliment. It was in passing. You know, is this seat taken? No. Do you mind if I sit here? No. I've never noticed this before, but you have exquisite lips.

JUNIE. Exquisite?

LASHLEY. Yeah, something like that.

JUNIE. Perfect. Even your lips are better. You know, Lashley, I don't know why you don't have a life because, Lord knows, if you wanted one, it's right there for the taking.

LASHLEY. What?

JUNIE. You have what it takes all over the place, in every area. So why you can't just reach out and take it is beyond me. Going off, having self-pity parties with a jug of alcohol. While the rest of us are left here actually trying.

LASHLEY. Jug? It was a sip. I only took one solitary sip.

JUNIE. Oh really, then what's this here bourbon all about?

(JUNIE *holds up a bottle of bourbon.*)

I have no respect for you. I'm done. Just go ahead and kiss Arthur Reid and Pastor Phil, drink till you pop at stupid sidewalk sales and end up on Mama's to-do list –

LASHLEY. I'm on Mama's to-do list?

JUNIE. *(Reading.)* "Remember to buy blackberry jam for Lashley."

LASHLEY. It says that?

JUNIE. Pastor Phil, if you will excuse me, I have a song to write and a poem to find.

(JUNIE *exits.*)

PASTOR PHIL. All I can think about is how I want to kiss you.

LASHLEY. So kiss me.

PASTOR PHIL. I got to go pray this through.

(**PASTOR PHIL** *exits.*)

LASHLEY. Let me know how that turns out.

(*Sparkley Clean Dry Cleaners.*)

(**JUNIE** *sings to her mom's picture.*)

[MUSIC NO. 11 "BEGIN AND END WITH YOU"]

JUNIE.

YOU WERE A SHOOTING STAR, BLAZING IN THE DARKNESS,
WITH A ONE-TRACK MIND AND A HEART OF STEEL.
SO YOU SET YOUR COURSE FOR BURNOUT OR GREATNESS,
DRIVEN BY THE THUNDER OF THOSE WHEELS.

(*Talking.*)

Hey, Mama. I sure do miss you and that voice of yours. I always thought you'd end up on a top ten record or in some celebrity magazine. But you never did. Makes me wonder do you ever think about coming back to us here?

(**LASHLEY** *family kitchen.*)

(**LYLE**, *still holding his box, sings to a picture of his wife. He stands in the doorway that leads into the kitchen.*)

LYLE.

I WAS A FRONT PORCH LIGHT, LEFT ON FOR A LONGING
THAT SOMEONE COULD COME MAKE MY HOUSE A HOME.
SO I STOOD MY GROUND, FOR LONELINESS OR PROMISE,
A FORTY-WATT HOPE AGAINST THE VAST UNKNOWN.

JUNIE.

OH, HOW COULD I HAVE KNOWN WHEN I WAS JUST A GIRL
THAT YOU'D GO AWAY?

(**LASHLEY** *sits at the kitchen table. She looks at the picture of her mother that hangs on the kitchen wall and sings.*)

LASHLEY.

AND I'VE SPENT SO MANY NIGHTS ON DREAMS OF YOU.

AND I

JUNIE & LASHLEY.

OFTEN WOKE BELIEVING YOU WERE DREAMING OF ME,
TOO.

LASHLEY.

BUT WHEN I FALL ASLEEP NOW

JUNIE & LASHLEY.

I DON'T KNOW WHAT I'M FALLING INTO.

JUNIE.

MAYBE I WAS JUST A FOOL FOR EVER HOPING IT WAS TRUE,
AND FOR LETTING ALL THE DREAMS I HAD BEGIN AND END
WITH YOU.
THIS HOLLOW-HEART IS CHANGING ME.

LASHLEY.

LIKE A THUNDERSTORM, IT RAINS IN ME.

LYLE.

AN ACHE THAT WON'T FADE LIKE IT SHOULD.

JUNIE.

SO, MAMA, COME BACK TO ME.

JUNIE & LASHLEY.

WHY DID YOU HAVE TO LEAVE?

JUNIE, LASHLEY & LYLE.

OH, PLEASE, COME BACK TO ME FOR GOOD.

LYLE.

AND WHEN I MET YOU I HAD DIFFERENT DREAMS COME
TRUE.

JUNIE & LASHLEY.

ALL THE THINGS I THOUGHT I WANTED ARE FADING OUT
OF VIEW.
AND I FEEL SO LOST, I CAN'T TELL WHAT I'VE FALLEN INTO.

JUNIE.

NOW, ALL THE DREAMS THAT I ONCE HAD BEGIN AND END
WITH YOU.

JUNIE & LASHLEY.

MAMA,

JUNIE, LASHLEY & LYLE.
ALL THE DREAMS I THOUGHT I HAD BEGIN AND END WITH
YOU.

End of Act One

ACT TWO

Scene One

(Third United Separated Harmony Church.)

(Arthur Reid funeral.)

(PASTOR PHIL *preaches.* **JUNIE, LASHLEY,** *and* **LYLE** *sit nearby.)*

PASTOR PHIL. A bell is simply a bell, till it is rung.

A song is simply a song, till it is sung.

And love doesn't grow in your heart to stay.

No, love isn't love till you give it...

to somebody...to somebody...to somebody.

(Holding up a piece of paper.)

This is Arthur Reid's life resume. He was a lawyer who fought for the rights of people...who were not lawyers. He coached the Hickory Hollow Chess and Archery Clubs. I know for a fact he saved, more than once, risked his life and literally saved turtles that were trying to cross Taradiddle Road. I am not the best pastor around. I know. So, when a good and giving man like Arthur Reid dies...

(Getting choked up.)

My first year seminary teacher used to always say, "God is more interested in our character than our happiness." Still, when a man, a turtle-saving, archery advocate, like Arthur Reid up and dies, all the answers ring hollow.

(Totally losing it.)

PASTOR PHIL. *(Cont.)* Sometimes, the answers just don't feel like sturdy, solid footing answers, you know?

> *(Unsure of what to do,* **JUNIE** *tries to rescue the moment.)*

JUNIE. That's right, Pastor Phil. God is way more interested in our character than our happiness.

LASHLEY. Although, I'm pretty sure God would like us to be happy.

JUNIE. Well said, Lashley. The joy of the Lord is my strength. This next song is called –

LASHLEY. *Thanks For The Naked Statue, Arthur.*

JUNIE. Now, Lashley. The statue my dear, sweet sister is referring to, *Ode To Humanity,* I think it's called –

LASHLEY. Oh, it's an ode all right –

JUNIE. It's a work of art, a tribute in bronze to all those –

LASHLEY. Naked people.

JUNIE. As many of you know Arthur Reid –

LASHLEY. Ellis, Arthur Ellis Reid.

JUNIE. Yes, Lashley, thank you for reminding us that the man had a middle name. Arthur… Ellis was the type of person who made beautiful, environmentally friendly things happen. And he may have sometimes given a few over-the-top compliments to some undeserving people here and…

> *(Gesturing toward* **LASHLEY.***)*

there. He also gave compliments to people who actually did deserve them.

> *(Looking heavenward.)*

This next song is for you, Arthur.

[MUSIC NO. 12 "ST. PETER, IF YOU'RE LISTENING, TELL ARTHUR REID HELLO"]

LASHLEY.

HE WAS A DO-GOODER, A GO-GETTER, AN ENERGIZER.

JUNIE.

HE INSPIRED US ALL FOR SURE.

LASHLEY.

HE WAS A TREE PLANTIN', PLANET-LOVIN' VEGAN.

JUNIE.

HIS LOVE FOR GOD WAS PURE.

*(**LASHLEY** interrupts with an unexpected musical riff.)*

LASHLEY.

OOOH! HE LOVED HIS LO-O-O-O-O-O-ORD-DAH!

JUNIE. He did. He really did love the One who thought up: camel, coyote and the red-lipped batfish.

LASHLEY & JUNIE.

SAINT PETER, IF YOU'RE LISTENIN', TELL ARTHUR REID HELLO.

JACOB, ISAAC, ABRAHAM, TELL HIM WE MISS HIM SO.

ANGELS, SHOW OUR FRIEND AROUND THROUGH THOSE STREETS OF GOLD.

SAINT PETER, IF YOU'RE LISTENIN', TELL ARTHUR REID HELLO.

JUNIE.

HE ALWAYS SAID, YOU HAVE TO WORK FOR PEACE.

LASHLEY.

IT WON'T DESCEND LIKE A MYSTICAL RAIN.

JUNIE.

HE DIED AN UNTIMELY DEATH –

LASHLEY. *(Interrupting.)*

CORN BREAD WAS TO BLAME.

JUNIE. It's true, he died of corn bread.

HE'S A NEWCOMER IN HEAVEN NOW AND –

LASHLEY. *(Interjecting.)*

ELLIS WAS HIS MIDDLE NAME.

LASHLEY & JUNIE.

SAINT PETER, IF YOU'RE LISTENIN', TELL ARTHUR REID HELLO.

MOSES, IF YOU HAVE THE TIME, TELL HIM WE MISS HIM SO.

WHY HE HAD TO LEAVE US, THE GOOD LORD ONLY KNOWS.
SAINT PETER, IF YOU'RE LISTENIN', TELL ARTHUR REID
  HELLO.

JUNIE.

HE BUILT THE ARCHIVE LIBRARY –

LASHLEY. *(Interrupting.)*

THOUGH NO ONE EVER GOES.

LASHLEY & JUNIE.

SAINT PETER, IF YOU'RE LISTENIN', TELL ARTHUR REID
  HELLO.

JUNIE. I just want to say that Arthur Reid was one of the finest square dancers a middle school girl could have the good fortune to do-si-do with. He was like sunshine with…ears.

> *(JUNIE abruptly exits.)*

PASTOR PHIL. As you can tell, we all feel strongly about Arthur Reid.

Only one life,

Will soon be past.

Only what's done

For love will last.

> *(Calling after mourners.)*

Oh, I forgot to mention, because our fellowship hall is undergoing a slight make-over, drinks and refreshments will be served inside Martha Urda's carport.

LASHLEY. I liked what you had to say about bells needin' to be rung and all. It was deep.

Scene Two

(Sparkley Clean Dry Cleaners.)

*(*JUNIE *listens to a* **LEAD SINGER INSTRUCTOR** *on the internet.)*

LEAD SINGER INSTRUCTOR. *(Voiceover.)* To be a lead singer, you must first discover what musical style best suits your unique voice and personality. Okay! Let's get started. Option one: yodeling.

[MUSIC NO. 13 "A LITTLE BITTY BUG"]

(Singing.)

A LITTLE BITTY BUG BIT A LITTLE BITTY BEAR.
A LITTLE BITTY BEAR DID SHE.

Your turn.

JUNIE.

A LITTLE BITTY BUG BIT A LITTLE BITTY BEAR.
A LITTLE BITTY BEAR DID SHE.

LEAD SINGER INSTRUCTOR. *(Voiceover.)* Doggone it, that was good! Now, try it faster.

(Singing.)

OH-DEL-OH-DEL-AY-EE-OO, OH-DEL-OH-DEL-AY-EE-EEE.

JUNIE.

A LITTLE BITTY BUG BIT A LITTLE BITTY BEAR
A LITTLE BITTY BEAR DID SHE.
OH-DEL-AY-EE-OO, OH-DEL-AY-EE-EEE.
YO-DEL-OH-DEL-AY-EE AI-DEL-OH-DEL-AY-EE OH-DEL-OH-DEL-AY-EE-EEE.
OH-DEL-OH-DEL-AY-EE-EE-EE-EEE.

Huh, I wonder if there's any money in yodeling.

LEAD SINGER INSTRUCTOR. Option two: maybe you're a punk rocker.

(Singing.)

WHY DID THE BUG BITE THE BEAR?
WHAT DID THE BEAR EVER DO?

Now, you.

JUNIE.

> WHY DID THE BUG BITE THE BEAR?
> WHAT DID THE BEAR EVER DO?

Ugh.

LEAD SINGER INSTRUCTOR. *(Voiceover.)* That was sick, Songbird, which is punk talk for "job well done." Option three: the blues. Think of something tragic.

> (**PASTOR PHIL** *enters with a box full of numerous flower arrangements.*)

PASTOR PHIL. Hey there, Junie.

JUNIE. Oh!

> *(Turning off Lead Singer Instruction and closing laptop.)*

Hey, Pastor Phil.

PASTOR PHIL. Do you want these flowers? The church is so jam packed with foliage, there's hardly any room left for the casket.

JUNIE. Won't the people that sent them notice that their flowers aren't over there?

PASTOR PHIL. I doubt it. Seriously, our little church can't handle this amount of horticulture.

JUNIE. I don't know, Pastor Phil.

PASTOR PHIL. Please, I want you to have them. Otherwise, I'll have to store them in the baptismal font.

JUNIE. They do smell nice.

PASTOR PHIL. Take them.

JUNIE. Okay, but only if you insist.

PASTOR PHIL. I insist.

> (**JUNIE** *takes the flowers.*)

JUNIE. I still can't believe poor Buzz Brisbee tripped on his own facial hair and died.

PASTOR PHIL. It was a long beard.

JUNIE. It was.

PASTOR PHIL. Talk about trials and tribulations. Buzz plus the Hattie C. Moore funeral will make it five deaths in the span of ten days.

JUNIE. I was already worried about my cholesterol level, but now I'm getting skittish when I even just brush my teeth.

PASTOR PHIL. I hear ya. This recent spate of dying has got me taking an extra vitamin C now and then my own self… Alrighty then, I better go and work some more on my eulogy.

JUNIE. Thanks for the flowers.

> (**PASTOR PHIL** *exits.* **JUNIE** *smells the flowers.*
> **LASHLEY** *enters.*)

LASHLEY. Junie, where's the ding-dang phone?

JUNIE. *(Showing off her flowers.)* Look what Pastor Phil gave to me.

LASHLEY. *(Reading a card.)* "The sound of your laughter will be missed"? These funeral flowers?

JUNIE. They are gifts that used to be condolences.

LASHLEY. In other words, he gave you some sloppy foliage seconds.

JUNIE. You know what, Lashley, my spleen's a little under the weather today. So, I'm not gonna argue with you about how Pastor Phil gave me not one, not two, but numerous flower bouquets.

LASHLEY. Your spleen is "under the weather"?

JUNIE. Yes, I've been having unexplained organ upheaval right around here all morning long.

> (**JUNIE** *waves her hand over her lung region.*)

LASHLEY. That's way too high to be something spleen oriented.

JUNIE. Our Buzz Brisbee funeral is gonna be packed. He was a bigwig in the music industry. So, this time, no corn bread comments and no naked people talk.

LASHLEY. Have you seen the phone?

JUNIE. Yes, 'cause I've been fielding calls all morning long, folks asking were you drunk at poor Arthur Reid's wake.

LASHLEY. I agreed to be a funeral singer, not a saint. Which reminds me. I been working on a number called *All You Can Eat Liver and Onions* for our upcoming funeral.

JUNIE. Say what?

LASHLEY. You said write about what the deceased liked and Buzz liked liver and onions.

JUNIE. First off, that is a terrible title. Secondly, we will be singing a song called *It's Good to Be in the Moment on Your Way to Forever.*

LASHLEY. Uh-huh. I was talking to his wife Melanie.

JUNIE. First wife. First wife.

LASHLEY. He was married to the woman for fifteen years. She should have some say in his funeral.

JUNIE. We're only getting song ideas from his current, last wife, wife number four.

LASHLEY. Destini was only with him eight months total. Besides, wives one through three had a lot to say about his lack of self-control and total obsession with model trains.

JUNIE. That's not the kind of information you bring up at a funeral.

LASHLEY. Why not?

JUNIE. Have you lost your only good mind?

LASHLEY. You're the one wanted me to be involved in the songwriting. Besides, I really like this *Liver* lyric. It's got a real message to it.

JUNIE. You are playing with fire.

LASHLEY. You're the one playing with fire.

(Reading one of the cards.)

"Our sorrow goes out to you and your family"? These flowers ain't nothing but a bunch of pollen-filled death fumes.

JUNIE. Death fumes?

LASHLEY. You've brought tragedy into the Sparkley.

JUNIE. Fine. I'll give them back. I wasn't up for hurtin' Pastor Phil's feelings, especially since my spleen was all inflamed, but fine.

LASHLEY. Just for the record, all that spleen upheaval you been having is probably from all that margarine you used to eat.

> (**LASHLEY** *exits.* **JUNIE** *looks at the flowers with fear and dread. Then, makes a phone call.*)

JUNIE. *(On phone.)* Dr. Milo? It's Junie again. What would you recommend to soothe a case of hyperspleenism? Chewable fish oil tablets. Sounds good. Well, not good, but thank you.

> (**JUNIE** *hangs up as she exits.*)

Scene Three

(Third United Separated Harmony Church.)

(Buzz Brisbee funeral.)

*(**LASHLEY** enters, early and drunk.)*

LASHLEY. Lovely, Ladies and Glamorous Gentlemen, you're my little early birdies. And as a special early birdie funeral treat, I'm thinking we should have a teeny tiny talk about our friend Buzz Brisbee. I'll go first.

[MUSIC NO. 14 "ALL YOU CAN EAT LIVER AND ONIONS"]

DOO DOO DOOT DOO DOO DOO DOOT DOOT.
DOO DOO DOOT DOO DOO DOO DOOT DOOT.
ALL THAT YOU CAN EAT LIVER AND ONIONS,
THAT WAS HIS FAVORITE MEAL.
HE LIKED GRAVY FROM A JAR,
HAD FIVE DOGS AND TEN CARS,
HE MADE RECORD DISTRIBUTION DEALS.
DOO DOO DOOT DOO DOO DOO DOOT.
HE SHOULDA BEEN SATISFIED WITH EIGHT KIDS AND
    THREE BRIDES,
BUT HE ALWAYS WANTED MORE.
HE LEFT HIS THIRD WIFE TO START A NEW LIFE,
AND BE THE OWNER OF A HOBBY STORE.
'CAUSE HIS LIFELONG GOAL, HIS NUMBER ONE HOPE,
HIS ALL-CONSUMING DESTINATION
WAS TO BE THE AT LARGE WORLDWIDE DIRECTOR
    DIRECTOR
OF THE NATIONAL MODEL RAILROAD ASSOCIATION.
I'M TALKIN' TRAINS. I'M TALKIN' MODEL TRAINS.

*(**JUNIE** enters.)*

JUNIE. What are you doing?

LASHLEY. Hey, Junie! We've all been singing a song about the truth together.

JUNIE. Please tell me you're not drunk.

LASHLEY. Okay. I will not tell you that.

JUNIE. You are totally out of line, Lashley.

LASHLEY. Not according to his first three wives I'm not.

JUNIE. We did not mutually agree to sing a song about the man's love for liver.

LASHLEY. Fine. You sing then. Go ahead, sing.

> (**JUNIE** *goes to sing, but can't.*)

I didn't think so. Now, sit down 'cause I got a killer bridge.

> (*To the mourners.*)

This part goes out to our dear ol' mother wherever she may be. Except for the train part.

> (**PASTOR PHIL** *enters with* **LYLE. LYLE,** *still carrying his box, takes a seat.*)

DO WHAT YOU WANT ON YOUR OWN TIME.
BUT YOU OUGHTA BE ASHAMED.
LEAVIN' YOUR LOVED ONES BEHIND,
BREAKIN' HEARTS AND CAUSIN' PAIN.

> (*To* **PASTOR PHIL.**)

You smell nice.

ALL FOR THE LOVE OF A MODEL TRAIN.

> (**LASHLEY** *seductively dances around* **PASTOR PHIL** *as she sings.*)

I'M TALKIN' CHA, CHA, CHA, CHA, CHA, CHA, CHA, CHA, CHA, CHA,
CHA, CHA, CHOO-CHOO TRAINS.
I'M TALKING CHA, CHA, CHA, CHA, CHA, CHA, CHA, CHA, CHA, CHA, CHA, CHA, CHOO-CHOO TRAINS.
CHOO-CHOO, CHOO-CHOO TRAINS.
CH-CH-CH-CHAA-CHAA, CHA-CHA, CH-CHAA-CHAA CHA CHA, CHA-CHA, CH-CHAA-CHAA,
CHEW-OOH TRAINS OOOOOH,
CHOO-CHOO, CHOW, CHOW, CHOW-CHOW-CHOW TRAINS.

PASTOR PHIL. Thank you, Lashley, you've given us all a lot to think about as we ponder the life of Buzz and his love of locomotion.

(**LASHLEY** *blows* **PASTOR PHIL** *a kiss.*)

PASTOR PHIL. *(Cont.)* Let's pray. May we all find a kettle for our chaos. May we all find calm within our haste. And within God's loving kindly cosmos, may we all feel embraced.

(**LASHLEY** *throws her arms around* **PASTOR PHIL** *as he prays.*)

Lord, help me, may we all feel embraced. Refreshments will be served at Uncle Bud's Fish House. Go in as much peace as possible.

(**PASTOR PHIL** *exits.*)

JUNIE. You are a walking disaster.

LASHLEY. You know what? I'm going to take that compliment and put it in my compliment bank.

JUNIE. That was not a compliment.

[MUSIC NO. 14A "VOCAL WARM UP"]

LASHLEY.
   BE BO BE BO BEE, GOOD MORNING, JUNIPER.

JUNIE. Drink a pot of coffee. We got our Hattie C. Moore funeral in less than three hours.

LASHLEY. I'm gotta go and practice.

(**LASHLEY** *exits.*)

JUNIE. Lashley, come back! Lashley! Lashley?

(**LYLE** *steps forward.*)

Hey, Daddy.

LYLE. At the bottom of River Road, there's a sharp curve. Promise me you won't go that way, okay, Maddy?

JUNIE. Okay, Lyle, I promise.

Scene Four

(Third United Separated Harmony Church.)

(Hattie C. Moore funeral.)

(**JUNIE** *stands at the podium.* **LYLE** *sits nearby holding his box.*)

JUNIE. *(Reading* **PASTOR PHIL***'s notes.)* Genesis fifty, verses nineteen through twenty. "Joseph said to them, 'Don't be afraid. Am I in the place of God? You intended to harm me, but God intended it for good to accomplish what is now being done.'" Right before she died, Hattie C. Moore said, and I quote, "I've had some hard knocks and some setbacks, but God used all of it for good."

(Sound of a door opening and closing.)

Lashley? Sorry 'bout that. I thought my sister would be here by now, but as it turns out Lashley is currently out of commission and Pastor Phil has flown the coop. As you all may know, I'm just the back-up singer. I'm the one sings the harmony part. Anyway, this song goes out to all you Hattie C. Moore fans...friends, family. It's based on some of her highs and lows and the experiences she experienced.

(**JUNIE** *sings the harmony part.*)

[MUSIC NO. 15 "ALCOHOLIC BUNGEE JUMPER"]

OOO, OOO, ALCOHOLIC.

AAAH, AAAH, BUNGEE JUMPER.

OO, OO, BAD MARRIAGE.

AH, AH, THREE GREAT KIDS.

(**JUNIE** *pauses as she listens to the lead vocal in her head.*)

MY LIFE COULD FILL THE PAGES OF A BOOK,

OH WHAT A BOOK!

BUT GOD MEANT IT ALL FOR GOOD.

GOD USED IT ALL FOR GOOD.

I'M NOT SURE HOW HE USED IT,
BUT I KNOW HE USED IT GOOD, YES.
GOD MEANT IT ALL FOR GOOD.
GOD USED IT ALL FOR GOOD.
THERE'S MEANING IN THE MEANING AND I KNOW HE
    MEANT IT–

      (**JUNIE** *whispers one, two, three, four, then sings…*)

GOOD.
OOO, OOO, TIME IN PRISON.
AAAH, AAAH, WROTE A NOVEL.
OO, OO, MET MY TRUE LOVE ON A HIKE.
AH, AH, LEARNED TO DRIVE AT SIXTY-FIVE.

      (**JUNIE** *pauses as she listens to the lead vocal in
      her head.*)

LIFE IS TOO SHORT, TOO DARN SHORT. LIFE IS TOO DARN
    SHORT.
BUT GOD MEANT IT ALL FOR GOOD.
GOD USED IT ALL FOR GOOD.
I'M NOT SURE HOW HE USED IT,
BUT I KNOW HE USED IT GOOD, YES.
GOD MEANT IT ALL FOR GOOD.
GOD USED IT ALL FOR GOOD.
THERE'S MEANING IN THE MEANING AND I KNOW HE
    MEANT IT–

      (**JUNIE** *whispers one, two, three, four then sings…*)

GOOD. GOOD. GOOD.

      (*While* **JUNIE** *talks to the congregation,* **LYLE** *looks
      in/finds a piece of paper in his box.*)

Refreshments and snacks are available in the newly
painted fellowship hall. Oh, just please don't touch the
walls. They're still wet.

      (**LYLE** *steps forward. He holds a death certificate.*)

LYLE. *(Upset.)* Maddy's gone. Maddy's gone.
JUNIE. It's okay, Daddy. It's okay.
LYLE. Maddy died.

JUNIE. *(Referring to the paper* **LYLE** *is holding.)* What you got there? Can I see it?

> **(JUNIE** *reads the death certificate.* **LYLE** *cries.)*

LYLE. My Maddy's gone.

JUNIE. Here, Daddy, let's sing. Wanna sing something?

> ### *[MUSIC NO. 16 "SWEET MACAROON (REPRISE)"]*

YOU'RE MY SWEET MACAROON, MY SWEET MACAROON.

JUNIE & LYLE.

MEET ME TONIGHT

JUNIE.

'NEATH THE

JUNIE & LYLE.

MOON, MY MACAROON,

LYLE.

YOU'RE MY

JUNIE & LYLE.

SWEET MACAROON.

LYLE.

MY

JUNIE & LYLE.

SWEET MACAROON.

MEET ME TONIGHT 'NEATH THE MOON, MY MACAROON.

Scene Five

(A crappy hotel room.)

(LASHLEY and PASTOR PHIL sit in a ratty bed.)

PASTOR PHIL. I wish I had met you before I met Midge.

LASHLEY. Are we gonna talk about your wife now?

PASTOR PHIL. Can you blame me? I'm a big cheat. I'm a cheater now.

LASHLEY. We didn't cheat.

PASTOR PHIL. We tried to.

LASHLEY. We kissed three times. And then you were so wracked with guilt about a wife who won't even take your phone calls, we stopped.

PASTOR PHIL. I'm sorry I brought up Midge.

LASHLEY. What kinda name is that?

PASTOR PHIL. A bad one.

LASHLEY. She's bigger than a house.

PASTOR PHIL. Not on the inside. On the inside, she's really very small.

LASHLEY. I refuse to feel guilty about this.

PASTOR PHIL. What do you think it'd been like if we'd gotten together, something like, fifteen or twenty years ago?

LASHLEY. I don't know.

PASTOR PHIL. Everything would have been the right temperature. Who knows? We coulda ended up anywhere, owning sheep maybe.

LASHLEY. Sheep?

PASTOR PHIL. Goats, dogs, salamanders.

LASHLEY. You're crazy.

PASTOR PHIL. I love how your smile reaches up into your eyeballs.

LASHLEY. I'm only smiling at the thought of salamanders.

PASTOR PHIL. Let's get married.

LASHLEY. You're already married.

PASTOR PHIL. They won't know that.

LASHLEY. And Midge?

PASTOR PHIL. That part's a problem.

LASHLEY. Yeah, she doesn't strike me as the divorcing type.

PASTOR PHIL. Which is crazy 'cause she's never gonna come back to me.

LASHLEY. *(Holding up a wine bottle.)* Want some?

PASTOR PHIL. I can't do that, I'm a pastor.

(There is a loud banging on the door.)

JUNIE. *(Offstage.)* Lashley? Lashley Lee Lashley?

PASTOR PHIL. Holy crap!

JUNIE. *(Offstage.)* I know you're in there.

PASTOR PHIL. How did she get here?

LASHLEY. I didn't want her to worry. So, I left a message.

JUNIE. *(Offstage.)* Lashley?

PASTOR PHIL. What did you say?

LASHLEY. I don't know. I was drunk. I could've said anything.

JUNIE. *(Offstage.)* Lashley!

PASTOR PHIL. Let me pretend to be counseling you?

LASHLEY. No.

JUNIE. *(Offstage.)* Lashley Lee Lashley!

LASHLEY. *(Opening the door.)* Junie! What are you doing here?

JUNIE. What do you mean what am I doing? I'm here to take you back.

*(Seeing **PASTOR PHIL**.)*

Oh.

PASTOR PHIL. Junie, I'm glad you've come. I'm here counseling. See, Lashley's here doing alcoholic beverages and the like and I'm trying to help.

JUNIE. Something 'bout that don't sound right.

PASTOR PHIL. A moment of weakness.

JUNIE. Why are your shoes off?

PASTOR PHIL. Huh?

LASHLEY. Just so you know, the good pastor and I have not had sex.

JUNIE. Just 'cause you're drunk and have impaired judgment, don't mean I do. Y'all are in a crappy hotel room with your shoes off in the middle of the day and we all know what that means.

PASTOR PHIL. *(Breaking down.)* I almost just had an affair and I'm in a terrible amount of debt.

JUNIE. You are a pastor! All we need is the faith of a mustard seed. Do you know how tiny a mustard seed is? How is it that you can't even maintain a mustard seed's worth of faith?

LASHLEY. Look, we're addicts.

JUNIE. Addict is just another word for selfish.

LASHLEY. Fine. I'm selfish. And, in a moment of total self absorption, I decided to buy some good wine and have a little fun.

JUNIE. Shut up, just shut the heck up.

LASHLEY. No, I won't just shut the heck up. You wake up humming, Junie. I wake up wanting more sleep, darker curtains. Just go on back home. I don't know why you came here anyway.

JUNIE. I came here 'cause I need to talk to you.

LASHLEY. I don't want to hear another one of your over-the-top pep talks, Junie.

JUNIE. Lashley –

LASHLEY. What?

JUNIE. You know how Daddy keeps talking about a sharp curve on River Road?

LASHLEY. Yes.

JUNIE. That's the place where Mama died.

LASHLEY. What are you talking about?

JUNIE. That's why I'm here. Mama died in a car wreck in Memphis.

LASHLEY. What?

JUNIE. Mama's death certificate was in that box Daddy's been carrying around.

(JUNIE *holds up the death certificate.*)

LASHLEY. She's been dead all along and Daddy just didn't tell us?

(JUNIE *holds up an old newspaper article.*)

JUNIE. I'm guessing he didn't want us to know that she died driving drunk.

LASHLEY. Where's Daddy?

JUNIE. Downstairs talking to the nice lady at the front desk.

LASHLEY. Does he know? Does he remember?

JUNIE. No.

LASHLEY. I'll come home in a day or so.

JUNIE. You're gonna keep on drinking?

LASHLEY. Yeah. I just found out my dad has been lying to me my entire life. So –

JUNIE. I'm sure he did it to protect us.

LASHLEY. If you don't mind, I came here to binge. And you are getting in the way of my buzz.

JUNIE. I can't leave you like this.

LASHLEY. Did you ever think that maybe I don't want you here?

JUNIE. But you're my sister.

LASHLEY. Just 'cause we're family don't mean we're friends.

JUNIE. Pastor Phil, are you coming or are you gonna stay here aiding and abetting and, no doubt, trying to seduce my good-hearted, dumb-ass sister?

PASTOR PHIL. I'm coming.

(JUNIE *exits with* PASTOR PHIL. *After a few seconds,* PASTOR PHIL *re-enters.*)

I left my shoes.

(Picking up his shoes.)

PASTOR PHIL. *(Cont.)* Don't give up on me, Lashley. I'll square things away with Midge, I promise.

LASHLEY. Please just go.

*(**PASTOR PHIL** exits.)*

Scene Six

(Lashley family kitchen.)

[MUSIC NO. 17 "HELLO TO ANOTHER GOODBYE"]

JUNIE.

I FEEL SO DISCONNECTED, EMPTY AND ALONE.
THIS IS NOT HOW I EXPECTED MAMA WOULD COME HOME.
AND NOW I'M COMING UNDONE.
I'M DRIFTING TOO FAR FROM THE SHORE.
ONLY TO FIND NOBODY'S HOME IN MY HEART ANYMORE.
LOVE ISN'T EVERYTHING, IT'S THE ONLY THING.
I SAID, LOVE ISN'T EVERYTHING, IT'S THE ONLY THING.
TURNS OUT THERE'S NO EASY ANSWERS. SOMETIMES,
    THERE'S NO WRONG OR RIGHT, I GUESS.
IT'S JUST HELLO TO ANOTHER GOODBYE.

> *(**LASHLEY** sings in the crappy hotel room. She holds up/sings to a bottle of wine.)*

LASHLEY. *(Holding up a wine bottle.)*

MY LONGEST RELATIONSHIP, MY BIGGEST REGRET.
THOUGHT I WAS OVER YOU, I GUESS NOT YET.
ALL ALONE IN THIS HOTEL ROOM WITH EMPTY BOTTLES
    OF WINE,

JUNIE & LASHLEY.

SOMEHOW I LOST MY WAY TO THE LIFE THAT WAS MINE.
LOVE ISN'T EVERYTHING, IT'S THE ONLY THING.

JUNIE.

I SAID,

JUNIE & LASHLEY.

LOVE ISN'T EVERYTHING, IT'S THE ONLY THING.
TURNS OUT THERE'S NO EASY ANSWERS. SOMETIMES,
    THERE'S NO WRONG OR RIGHT, I GUESS.
IT'S JUST HELLO TO ANOTHER GOODBYE.

> *(**LYLE** sings in The Sparkley Clean Dry Cleaners and **PASTOR PHIL** sings in the Third United Separated Harmony Church.)*

EVERYONE.

ONE OF THESE SOMEDAYS,

LASHLEY.

I'LL GIVE YOU UP FOR GOOD.

LYLE.

SHE'LL COME BACK TO ME.

LASHLEY, LYLE & PASTOR PHIL.

ONE OF THESE SOMEDAYS,

JUNIE.

I'LL GET THE LIFE THAT I WANT.

PASTOR PHIL.

I WILL FINALLY BREAK FREE.

EVERYONE.

WHY DO I KEEP ON WAITING FOR CHANGE TO COME TO ME
SOMEDAY?

WHY NOT NOW?

JUNIE.

LOVE ISN'T EVERYTHING, IT'S THE ONLY THING. I SAID,

JUNIE & LASHLEY.

LOVE ISN'T EVERYTHING, IT'S THE ONLY THING.

JUNIE.

OH,

JUNIE, LASHLEY & PASTOR PHIL.

LOVE ISN'T EVERYTHING, IT'S THE ONLY THING.

EVERYONE.

TURNS OUT THERE'S NO EASY ANSWERS, SOMETIMES
THERE'S NO WRONG OR RIGHT.

I GUESS IT'S JUST HELLO

JUNIE.

TO ANOTHER

EVERYONE.

HELLO,

JUNIE.

TO ANOTHER

EVERYONE.

HELLO,

JUNIE.

TO ANOTHER GOODBYE.

> *(Sound of a hard rain beginning to fall.)*
>
> *(**LYLE** enters the kitchen.)*

LYLE. Hey, Honey Bunch.

JUNIE. Daddy, it's me, Junie.

LYLE. I know.

JUNIE. You do?

LYLE. Of course, I do.

JUNIE. *(Hugging her dad.)* Oh, Daddy! It's so good to see you.

LYLE. Well, it's good to see you too.

JUNIE. Can I get you something? Are you hungry?

> *(Sound of thunder.)*

LYLE. Listen to that rainstorm. I always loved the sound of thunder.

JUNIE. I hope no trees crash through the roof and fall on us.

LYLE. Yeah, that would be a fairly tragic turn of events. I met your mama on a rainy night like this.

JUNIE. Yeah?

LYLE. I had a brave and ridiculous crush on this redheaded cellist named Joleen Piper. Anyway, I went over to her apartment for dinner. Homemade pizza, I think it was. Maddy was her roommate. And, throughout the meal, Maddy talked to me non-stop while that Joleen Piper barely said a word and then the darn girl vanished like an apparition into her room. It would've been incredibly disappointing were it not for Maddy's unwavering attention. She asked could I drive her to the library. And on the way, it began to pour buckets and buckets of rain. Suddenly, she said, "Stop the car." And there, at the War Memorial, overlooking all of downtown Nashville, we danced.

JUNIE. I've missed you, Daddy.

LYLE. Hard day?

JUNIE. Terrible. It's just, nothing is the way I thought it would be. What I mean is, I'm not really sure how I got here. Not to the house, of course, but here to this time line, because the path I'm on doesn't look familiar to me in the tiniest little bit. It isn't the path I pictured myself on at all.

LYLE. What's the one thing you want most?

JUNIE. All I ever wanted was to be a lead singer, really.

LYLE. In that case, here look, just stand up and sing.

> (JUNIE *stiffly stands up.*)

JUNIE. I can't do it. When I stand up to sing by myself, I just panic. I'm not the lead singer type.

LYLE. Try and unlock your arms from your sides.

> (*She awkwardly holds her arms away from her body.*)

JUNIE. It's no use. I'm a natural born side arm locker. I shouldn't have brought it up.

LYLE. Junie.

JUNIE. I'll just keep on singin' the harmony part.

LYLE. You can't quit. We barely just started.

JUNIE. I feel like a first rate fool.

LYLE. Oh, good lord, Juniper. Just let the music take you to another place.

> **[MUSIC NO. 18 "LAY YOUR BURDEN DOWN"]**

> (*Singing.*)

OH, SHADRACH, MESHACH, ABEDNEGO, IN THE FIERY FLAMES WERE TOSSED,
WHEN THEY COMMENCED TO PRAYIN' TO THE ALMIGHTY BIG BOSS.
NEBUCHADNEZZAR DROPPED HIS JAW WHEN HE PEEKED RIGHT IN,
AN ANGEL RIGHT THERE IN THEIR MIDST AND NARY A HAIR WAS SINGED.

NOW IF THE LORD COULD BRING THOSE POOR BOYS
    THROUGH THE FIRE,
MAYBE EVEN YOU AND ME CAN HEAR THAT ANGEL CHOIR
SINGIN', LAY YOUR BURDEN, LAY IT DOWN, LAY IT RIGHT ON
    DOWN.
SEND THOSE PRAYERS UP TO THE LORD AND LAY YOUR
    BURDEN DOWN!

    (Speaking.)

Now you try.

JUNIE. Daddy.

LYLE. Just think of it as a conversation. Like this.

LAST NIGHT I HAD CAULIFLOWER AND THIS MORNIN' I HAD
    GAS.

JUNIE. I'm not singin' about gas.

LYLE. Just tell the folks the situation.

THESE DAYS, I GET UP THREE TIMES A NIGHT JUST TO GO
    PEE.
AND OFTEN, ONCE I GET WOKE UP, I CAN'T GET BACK TO
    SLEEP.
IT'S FUNNY WHAT YOU THINK ABOUT IN THE SILENCE OF
    THE NIGHT.
AND IT'S HARD TO TELL THE DIFFERENCE BETWEEN
    DREAMS AND REAL LIFE.
I'VE HAD HALF A HEART SINCE THE DAY YOUR MAMA LEFT.
NOW IT SEEMS MY MIND IS GOIN' TOO.
YOU GOTTA

JUNIE. *(Singing the harmony part.)*

LAY YOUR BURDEN, LAY IT DOWN, LAY IT RIGHT ON DOWN.

JUNIE & LYLE.

SEND THOSE PRAYERS UP TO THE LORD AND LAY YOUR
    BURDEN DOWN!

LYLE. Take the lead now, Junie. Just pretend you're singing
back-up, but sing the lead part.

JUNIE. Alright.

YESTERDAY, I HAD MYSELF A TUNA MELT ON WHEAT.

LYLE. That's it.

JUNIE.

> IT HAD THE PERFECT BALANCE OF CHEESE AND MELT AND
> MEAT.
> JUST WHEN I PREPARED TO DIP THAT SANDWICH IN MY
> SOUP,
> I SAW RIGHT THERE A FLOATIN' HAIR, AND I HAD TO
> REGROUP.
> EVERY TIME MY HOPES GET UP, AND I THINK I'M ON THE
> RISE,
> THE RUG GETS PULLED RIGHT OUT FROM UNDER ME!
>> *(Singing harmony part.)*
> LAY MY BURDEN, LAY IT DOWN, LAY IT RIGHT ON DOWN.
> SEND THOSE PRAYERS UP TO THE LORD AND LAY YOUR
> BURDEN DOWN!

LYLE. Sing the second verse the way your mama woulda
sung it.

JUNIE. *(Gaining courage as she goes.)*

> OLD JOB LOST NEAR EVERYTHING, HIS LAND, HIS SHEEP,
> HIS WEALTH.
> HE EVEN LOST HIS FAMILY. HE EVEN LOST HIS HEALTH.
> ALL HE HAD WAS FAITH, SO HE LET OUT A LOUD PRAYER
> CRY.
> THE BIG G SENT HIS MERCY DOWN, RESTORIN' OLD JOB'S
> LIFE.
> IF JOB COULD STILL CALL OUT, WHEN HE'D LOST
> EVERYTHING,
> THEN I CAN OVERCOME MY FEAR, OPEN MY MOUTH AND
> SING!
> YOU'VE GOTTA... YOU'VE GOTTA...
> LAY YOUR BURDEN DOWN. LAY IT RIGHT ON DOWN.
> SEND THOSE PRAYERS UP TO THE LORD AND LAY YOUR
> BURDEN,
> LAY THAT BURDEN, LAY THAT BURDEN DOWN, DOWN,
> LAY THAT BURDEN DOW – NAH!
>> **(JUNIE** *hugs* **LYLE,** *but* **LYLE** *back in an*
>> *Alzheimer's state no longer remembers who she is.)*

Thank you, Daddy!

LYLE. You're welcome.

JUNIE. When you told me to sing like Mama, something inside me just clicked.

(Pause.)

Speaking of Mama…

(Pause.)

Daddy, why didn't you tell us that Mama died?

LYLE. Your mother died? I'm sorry to hear that, Young Lady.

JUNIE. No, Daddy, it's me Junie.

LYLE. That's funny. We have a daughter named Junie.

JUNIE. You do? Wanna tell me about her?

LYLE. Of course! She looks just like her mama and she's the brightest ray of sunshine you ever did meet.

*(**LYLE** talks to **JUNIE** as they exit.)*

Scene Seven

(Third United Separated Harmony Church.)

(Maddy Louisa Lashley funeral.)

*(**LASHLEY** enters and talks to her mother's urn.)*

LASHLEY. Hey, Mama, it's me Lashley. Wish me luck. After your funeral, I'm going back to rehab. This idea that this whole time I haven't been abandoned…it's re-writing my entire life. Truth is, I'm so used to feeling abandoned, I don't know how else to feel.

*(Having overheard, **JUNIE** enters.)*

JUNIE. It's like we've lived our whole life backwards.

LASHLEY. Yeah.

JUNIE. You know, every day, since the day Mama went away, I woke up wondering would this be the day she came back? I just always felt like the thing that was missing inside had to do with her. Thinkin' if I just had Mama back or a successful singin' career, I'd finally feel like a big deal somebody.

Now, I come to find out, I either feel like a big deal somebody or I don't.

(Full of wonder.)

Mama didn't leave us.

*(**JUNIE** bursts into laughter.)*

Mama loved us all along.

*(The two sisters laugh and hug. **PASTOR PHIL** enters with **LYLE**. **LYLE** takes his seat. **PASTOR PHIL** gives the eulogy.)*

PASTOR PHIL. Today, we are here to celebrate the life of Maddy Louisa Lashley.

LYLE. That's my wife's name. She'll be here shortly.

JUNIE. Let's let the nice man speak, okay, Daddy?

LYLE. Whatever you say, Young Lady.

PASTOR PHIL. Hoping to make his daughters' lives stable,

(Referring to **LYLE**.*)*

my friend here bottled up his pain along with his wife's remains in this here urn.

Meanwhile, the girls kept hoping she'd return. While all the while, their mother sat right there on a nearby table.

We all have secrets that we sometimes keep. My friend over there kept his wife's death a secret. Was it a good choice? I am not the right one to ask, for I myself have been a wolf in sheep's clothing. I've been a wolf in sheep's clothing.

LYLE. Sounds hot.

PASTOR PHIL. And now, Junie would like to say a few words. Junie?

(**JUNIE** *steps forward.*)

JUNIE. Thank you, Pastor Phil. Recently, I came across a list of my mama's mundane chores. *Remember to Buy Blackberry Jam for Lashley, Knit a Hat for Junie So She Won't Catch Cold, This Haircut Works,* which I'm pretty sure was about a mullet she got once. Then, after a whole lotta searchin', I found this, my mama's music book.

(Holding up a book of notated music.)

And I come to find out that that list of chores was actually a list of lyrics that she'd been writin' for me and my sister. That said, I'd like to ask my sister Lashley to come up here so we can sing y'all a tune from our Mama's songbook, called *A Poem for My Daughters.*

LASHLEY. Mama wrote us a song?

JUNIE. A whole album's worth of songs.

(Reading from the songbook.)

To Junie and Lashley, written with all my love, Mama.

[MUSIC NO. 19 "TO BUILD A BEAUTIFUL LIFE"]

JUNIE.
    YOU GOTTA DIE TO LIVE, LET GO TO HOLD ON.

YOU GOTTA STOP SINGIN' TO LEARN THE SONG.

TURN IT ON ITS END, IT'S NOT WHAT YOU THINK.

IF YOU WANNA FIND A BRIDGE, YOU GOTTA GO TO THE
BRINK.

IT'S AN UPSIDE DOWN MERRY-GO-ROUND.

YOU GOTTA DIG DEEP TO GET UPWARD BOUND.

I KNOW YOU DON'T THINK YOU CAN, BUT YOU CAN.

JUNIE & LASHLEY.

I KNOW YOU DON'T THINK YOU ARE, BUT YOU ARE.

'CAUSE THERE'S LOVE TO FIND IF YOU WANT TO BE FOUND.

LASHLEY.

IF YOU WANNA SAIL THE SKIES, YOU GOTTA WALK ON THE
GROUND.

TO GET WHAT YOU WANT, YOU GOTTA LAY IT DOWN.

START AT THE END, AND WORK BACKWARD FROM THERE.

IF YOU DON'T KNOW WHERE YOU ARE, HOW CAN YOU GET
ANYWHERE?

JUNIE & LASHLEY.

IT'S AN UPSIDE DOWN MERRY-GO-ROUND.

GOTTA DIG DEEP TO GET UPWARD BOUND.

I KNOW YOU DON'T THINK YOU CAN, BUT YOU CAN.

I KNOW YOU DON'T THINK YOU ARE, BUT YOU ARE.

'CAUSE THERE'S LOVE TO FIND IF YOU WANT TO BE FOUND.

JUNIE.

YOU STACK ONE MORE DAY ON TOP OF ONE MORE NIGHT.

IT TAKES A LOTTA SMALL STEPS TO BUILD A BEAUTIFUL
LIFE.

JUNIE.	**LASHLEY.**
YOU STACK ONE MORE DAY ON TOP OF ONE MORE NIGHT.	YOU STACK ONE MORE DAY ON TOP OF ONE MORE NIGHT.
IT TAKES A LOTTA SMALL STEPS	IT TAKES A LOTTA SMALL STEPS
TO BUILD A BEAUTIFUL LIFE.	TO BUILD A BEAUTIFUL LIFE.
JUNIE & LASHLEY.	**PASTOR PHIL & LYLE.**
YOU STACK ONE MORE DAY	IT TAKES A LOTTA SMALL STEPS

ON TOP OF ONE MORE
   NIGHT.
IT TAKES A LOTTA SMALL
   STEPS
TO BUILD A BEAUTIFUL
   LIFE.

TO BUILD A BEAUTIFUL
   LIFE.
YOU STACK ONE MORE DAY

ON TOP OF ONE MORE
   NIGHT.

    *(**LASHLEY, LYLE,** and **PHIL** continue to sing the round as* **JUNIE** *sings the following…)*

JUNIE.
   THERE IS… LOVE TO… FIND IF… YOU WANT TO.

LASHLEY.

YOU STACK ONE MORE DAY

ON TOP OF ONE MORE
   NIGHT.
IT TAKES A LOTTA SMALL
   STEPS
TO BUILD A BEAUTIFUL
   LIFE.

PASTOR PHIL & LYLE.

IT TAKES A LOTTA SMALL
   STEPS
TO BUILD A BEAUTIFUL
   LIFE.
YOU STACK ONE MORE DAY

ON TOP OF ONE MORE
   NIGHT.

EVERYONE.
   I KNOW YOU DON'T THINK YOU CAN, BUT YOU CAN.
   I KNOW YOU DON'T THINK YOU ARE, BUT YOU ARE.
   'CAUSE THERE'S LOVE TO FIND IF YOU WANT TO BE FOUND.

End of Play

PROPERTY LIST

One handheld microphone
One microphone in a mic stand
Neck brace
Radio
A book titled *Starting Over After Falling Apart*
A counter
Hangers
Stapler
Wrinkled pants
A purple polyester ochre jacket with a missing button
Numerous men's shirts
Two large framed pictures of Maddy
One small picture of Maddy
Toaster
Bread
Cereal
Milk
Spoon, butter knife, saucer
Margarine
Trash can
Lashley's robe
Lashley's cell phone
Lashley Sister's bank statement for $1.68
Numerous small appliances including two electric juicers
A small manual, plastic citrus juicer
Unopened bottle of bourbon
Junie's aquamarine dress
Pastor Phil's suit jacket
Lashley's purse
Pastor Phil's cell phone
Daily Racing Form
Bindy Moss' food drive shirt
Plate of food (radishes with meat and egg jello)
Numerous cardboard boxes
Lyle's small cardboard box
Maddy's yard work hat
Maddy's special occasion dress
Maddy's robe

Two pieces of torn paper that read, "a poem for my daughters" (one for robe pocket, one for box)

A pack of old peppermints

Lyle and Maddy's song set list

Junie's dog ears for Jimmy Boy Brown funeral (easy to put on and off)

Junie's small cardboard box

A piece of paper that reads "This haircut works"

A piece of paper that reads, "Remember to buy blackberry jam for Lashley"

A torn piece of paper that reads "Someday maybe I'll write" (this should fit together with the paper that reads "a poem for my daughters"

A wad of cash

Arthur Reid's life resume

A 2008 laptop computer

A box of funeral flower arrangements with cards that read, "The sound of your laughter will be missed" and "Our sorrow goes out to you and your family"

Business phone for Sparkley Clean Dry Cleaners

Pastor Phil's eulogy notes for Buzz Brisbee funeral

Maddy's death certificate

Newspaper article about Maddy's drunken car wreck

A half-empty wine bottle

An urn

Maddy's scored/notated songbook